Alias Podge

Wendy Long

Illustrations by
Rosalind Stafford

𝕯

DELISLE

LONDON & SHERBORNE

Published by Delisle Limited
6 Broad Street Place, London, E.C.2

All Editorial and Trade Correspondence to:
Delisle Limited, Cromwell House, Sherborne, Dorset

First Edition . . . December 1965

This book is set in 11 on 13 pt. Garamond and printed by
Blackie & Son Limited, Bishopbriggs, Glasgow

To my friends of the Vale
who variously inspired and made this possible
and above all to my Parents
this book is gratefully
and affectionately dedicated.

Contents

I

The Farm

In which Podge arrives and meets Minnie and Manager

HIS real name was Magpie, but he was always known as Podge. He came from a very aristocratic family indeed. They were hunt terriers of a rather special kind, and they were very proud of their Family and its history. He had been called Magpie because of his colour, which like that of his relations was mostly white, with a black head (except for the lopsided white streak from his forehead to his nose), a black patch on his shoulder, a black saddle-shaped mark on his back and a black tail. He was very smart, and the black patches had clear outlines and stood out distinctly from the white. His family, who thought that neatness and tidiness were important, were proud of such a tidy-looking puppy, even though he was a bit solid. Still, plumpness is to be expected in puppies. It was only when he began to get bigger and taller without getting thinner that he acquired the nickname of Podge; and that was the name which stuck.

His family in fact didn't see him getting older and taller but not any thinner (nor would they have dreamed of referring to him, even in jest, as Podge), for as soon as he was old enough to leave his mother he was sent away to live with some relations who lived on a farm half a mile away across the fields (it might just as well have been ten for all Podge knew: only when he grew up did he discover how close he was to his family home, and what possibilities this offered). It was a bit like the custom long ago of noblemen sending their children to live with other families so that they could be taught manners and all the other important things they would need to know when they were grown up.

He was taken to the farm one evening, and introduced to the farmer and his wife and children. They gave him some bread and milk, and then they took him out of the

house and across the yard and put him in a barn. Then they patted him and left him, and he could see the door of the farmhouse close and the light disappear abruptly.

He was rather bewildered and a little lonely. He looked around him, and saw overhead old wooden rafters and the underneath of the old stone tiles, and on three sides grey stone walls, weathered and rough. On the fourth side the barn was open, with a gate across it to keep out the cows. It was filled with bales of hay, and between them and behind them and on top of them were hollows which were just the right size for a smallish dog, and in which he could curl up and be warm at night. The hay smelt very sweet, especially in the evening when the air was cool and soft.

Podge staggered up onto his fat paws and began to look round. At first he could only see the bales of hay inside and the darkness outside. The yard seemed very big and rather frightening, and the buildings round it showed as dark and mysterious shadows. It seemed very quiet, too, after the constant noises of his family home, where dogs and people and horses were coming and going and talking and arguing and joking all the time.

Gradually he began to hear more noises, and he realized that he was not so alone as he had thought. There were small rustling sounds in the hay which he couldn't identify; there were faint hoots of owls and twitterings of swallows; there was the noise of a horse stamping and blowing down its nose as it stood nearby tied to the gate; and there was the sound of paws approaching.

Two pairs of eyes appeared out of the darkness, and as they came nearer Podge could see the outlines of the two dogs they belonged to. One was large and white. He had a long rough coat and black markings not unlike Podge's own. He looked at Podge in a rather off-handed manner and said:

'Well, I suppose we shall have to put up with the inconvenience.'

The other dog, who was shorter, with a long soft brown coat, white legs and enormous eyes overarched by long eyebrows, frowned at him, and came across the pile of bales to where Podge stood.

'Poor podgy puppy,' she said. 'Did you think you were alone?'

The other dog snorted; but her words had the intended effect upon Podge, who immediately felt reassured and let her curl up beside him and lick his coat just as his mother had used to. She went on talking busily out of the corner of her mouth and in between licks to the white dog, who was carefully making himself comfortable on a nearby bale.

'Well,' she said, 'Of course, when she told me that They were sending him here I told her straight that I didn't think it was right for rich folks to send their puppies away from home and have other people do all their work for them. I mean, I don't think it's fair to the puppy, do you, Manager? I mean, when he grows up he won't know his family like he should and it stands to reason he won't settle down there, doesn't it? But I told her we'd do our best for him, and train him up properly.'

'You always get so worked up about these things, Minnie,' said the white dog impatiently, carefully cleaning between his pads. 'Talk, talk, talk, all the time. Now, I spent this morning helping Him with the harrowing. That's what matters at this time of year, now, not gossiping with Flossie at the Lodge. They wouldn't feel the same without me running beside the tractor all the way, or sitting on top of the trailer to bring it back safely. Why, He said to me only this morning, "You're a good dog, Manager, a good dog." '

'Hm,' said Minnie. 'Well, *They* will be grateful to you, never mind *Him*, if we bring the puppy up properly. Personally, I know what comes first and what matters most, even if you don't. You may think that the whole farm depends on you if you like, though I think it just possibly might get along without you; but don't you see that this is our big chance to prove our interests aren't just—just *insular*. There are wider horizons than the farm, you know,' she finished triumphantly.

Manager sniffed contemptuously. Whatever insular meant, he was sure Minnie was as bad as he. However, he did secretly feel flattered that they had been entrusted with the job of bringing up the puppy from the Great House. It was a considerable honour—though he would never admit to Minnie that he thought so.

Podge had given up trying to understand, and had fallen asleep with his square nose on his large blunt paws, sighing heavily from time to time. Minnie gave a few finishing licks to his coat, and then curled up beside him for the night. Manager selected a hay-bale which gave him a commanding view of the whole yard and part of the lane, so that he could see anyone approaching, and sat there dozing, keeping one eye half-open and one ear cocked to catch any suspicious sound.

Presently the farmer, doing his rounds before going to bed, looked in to see how the puppy was. Manager thumped his tail vigorously to tell him everything was

fine, and Minnie opened one sleepy eye in recognition. Podge didn't wake. The farmer went in and told his wife that it would be all right. Then he took his boots off and went to bed.

2

Ratting

In which Podge is taught an ancient skill

O Podge's life at the farm began, and he soon forgot the kennels where he had been born and thought of the farm as his home. As he got bigger he began to explore; and, being curious, he was always getting into trouble. He found that sour cream was put out for the pigs, and had several accidents with buckets that fell over as he was stealing from them and poured cream all over him. He found that eggs tasted very nice, and was frequently smacked for breaking them. He was always getting covered with mud and muck while exploring, and had to spend a lot of time cleaning himself under Minnie's strict supervision ('A terrier is a *tidy* dog!').

He used to tease the cows by running behind them and under them and snapping at their heels as they stood in the stall waiting to be milked, but they refused to take any notice; and he often made Minnie very cross by pretending to attack her when she wasn't expecting it. He would stalk her round the garden and then jump at her, growling, or hide behind a bush or a cabbage plant as she went by and then bark suddenly to make her jump.

'That puppy's too full of hisself,' she complained

7

crossly to Manager after one of these incidents. 'Needs discipline, that's what!'

'Never you fret,' said Mangaer patiently. 'It's only natural in a puppy his age. Something will turn up to take his mind off it, you'll see.'

And something did happen, just as Manager had said. One day when Podge was about six months old Minnie, Manager and he were sitting out in the yard, warming themselves in the afternoon sun and snapping lazily at flies when they came too close. Minnie was washing herself and Manager was chewing over an old bone which he had found. Podge lay flat on his side between them. Suddenly the door of the farm-house opened, and two of the farmer's children came rushing out, clutching large, thick sticks. They had just come home from school, had their tea and thankfully changed from their uniforms into old and battered jeans; and they looked purposeful.

'Come on Min! Manager—here! Come on, Podge, old boy!'

'This means business,' said Manager, getting to his feet and stretching himself—first his front legs and then his back ones. Minnie stood up and shook her long fur into place.

'Rats,' she said meaningfully. 'Pay attention, puppy, this is *important*.'

They followed the children eagerly through the gate-way at the back of the yard and went between the hay-ricks to one of the large chicken-houses behind them. Podge had never been allowed inside one of these before, though he had once tried to go in when the farmer's wife was feeding the hens, and had been smacked and shut out. Altogether, hens were a bad bet, it seemed, for when he

8

had chased one one day when it came strutting into the yard Minnie had scolded him:

'Don't lower yourself by chasing *them*,' she had said; but she didn't explain what she meant.

The children opened the hen-house door. This time there were no fluttering, squawking hens inside—it was empty; but as the door opened there were sinister rustlings in the straw, which stopped abruptly. They all climbed up the two steps outside and went in, and the door was shut. The shed was rather dark, even though it was still quite light outside, so that the huge torch which the children carried was put in one corner, where it cast some bright light and some very dark shadows in the corner and from the big low beams that went across the shed supporting the pointed roof.

'Wait here,' said Minnie, and Podge sat down just beside the door, nervous and excited but absolutely still. The children went down to the end of the shed, and stood at each side, clutching their thick sticks to catch any rats that came their way.

Then Minnie and Manager worked their way down one side of the shed. Minnie ferreted around in the straw in

the corners and where the walls joined the floor, sniffing at all the holes she remembered, while Manager stood a little farther out, watching her intently, poised ready to pounce. They had gone a little way when Minnie suddenly gave a little bark and started trotting quickly along, with her nose to the ground. Manager waited, completely still apart from his tail which was quivering with excitement.

Then the rat broke cover and made a dash for it. He rushed out and headed across the shed. Manager wasn't quite quick enough. He pounced but just missed, and the rat dived safely into a hole in the opposite wall.

'Oh, my whiskers!' said Minnie impatiently. 'You're losing your grip!'

'Nonsense,' said Manager, rather cross that the puppy had seen him miss it. 'No-one could possibly have caught it—it was much too fast—like lightning it was.'

Minnie wasn't listening. She had already begun sniffing amd poking again.

Podge was terrifically excited. He had never seen a rat before though he had often been told about them—how big they were, how strong, how fast and how nasty. Minnie had often told him what horrid habits rats had, and how all terriers were their natural enemies. He felt a proper hatred of them; but at the same time he was a bit afraid. The thick tail, especially, made him feel rather sick. This rat had looked as if it was employed in evil things, its whiskers had twitched in a most unpleasant manner, and though it was obviously in a very tight spot it hadn't really looked afraid, only contemptuous.

By this time Minnie had found the scent of another, and had driven it out from its hole behind a pile of old nesting-boxes stacked up against the wall. It ran, very fast, down the length of the hen-house, searching for some way of escape. Then it saw the children waiting at the end, and in desperation swerved away, out across the shed. Manager had been waiting for this, crouched low

in the straw, and as it came across, half-looking over its shoulder at Minnie and not realizing he was there, he made a sudden leap and caught it. It was all over in a second, almost before Podge had had time to blink.

'Oh, *good* dog!' cried the children, running up to Manager and thumping him on the back. 'That *was* clever of you! And good old Min, too.' Manager and Minnie stood side by side, grinning and wagging their tails furiously, congratulating themselves on their team-work. 'Now you see how it's done,' they said to Podge. 'It's nothing, really, just a matter of timing.'

'I want to try,' said Podge. 'Please let me—I'll be very quiet, and when it comes I'll *pounce*—wham!—like this!' He sprang and with tremendous force bowled Minnie over.

She picked herself up, her coat full of straw, and batted him smartly with a fore-paw. 'That was unnecessary and most inappropriate,' she said severely. 'Business is business and must be taken seriously. You're here to learn, not to show off.'

Podge felt rather ashamed. 'Sorry,' he grunted. 'I got carried away.'

The children were roaring with laughter at all this, and the dogs felt embarrassed. With great dignity and self-importance they took up their positions for the next hunt, but their stiffness and injured dignity only made the children laugh even more.

This time Podge was sent up onto one of the big beams. It wasn't very far above the ground, and it was quite easy to climb up by means of the various ledges and struts along the wall. At the other end, just opposite to him, were more nesting boxes in a row below the beam. It seemed a long way off, and the beam seemed to him to get narrower the farther away it got, though at this end it was quite wide enough for him to crouch safely on.

He waited, tense and expectant, twitching his stubby tail, while Manager and Minnie approached the boxes in a sort of pincer movement from opposite directions, ferreting busily around, sniffing in the straw and talking in brisk, staccato barks as they did so.

'Nothing in this one.'

'Old scent here.'

'Immense one here last year, remember?'

'Ah, that's better. Scent quite recent. Going your way.'

'Yes, got it—now then, my beauty . . .'

And as Manager spoke the rat—rather a small one—shot out of the box like a bullet and, seeing that there was no way out down below, took the only way open and ran up onto the beam.

Podge saw the movement and flattened himself close against the beam in the dark shadows so that the rat wouldn't see him till the last possible moment. It ran

along the beam, not really hurrying as it could see its enemies below and thought it was safe. As it came nearer Podge could see its little eyes gleaming and hear its thick tail trailing in the dust. And he could smell its horrible rat-smell.

Suddenly he found that he was angry—very angry indeed with this nasty beast which had invaded the hen-house, where it had no business to be, which lived on rubbish and decaying things, which liked dirt, and which never did anything to help the farm. There was another side to his anger, though—the sheer unthinking hate for rats bred into terriers over hundreds of years.

Filled with this anger he waited, every muscle tense, ready to spring, waited until the rat was very close and he could hear its quick breathing. Then he made one gigantic lunge, putting all his strength and weight into it.

Podge and the dead rat tumbled to the ground to-gether. Podge naturally curled up and rolled over as he landed, and hardly noticed the fall. He got to his feet, ready to attack again, and was almost surprised to see that the rat wasn't moving, that he had managed it first go. He was tremendously pleased with himself.

So were the others. The children came running up to pat him. 'Golly,' they said, 'He'll be a great ratter one day—just like Manager. He *was* quick, wasn't he! Well done, Podge! *Good* old dog then!'

'Not bad at all,' said Manager gruffly.

Minnie chose this moment to be dignified. She coughed apologetically and shifted her feet, like someone beginning to make a speech, and said:

'Yes, that really was well done, Magpie,' (using his formal name). 'Your Family would have been proud of you. You are carrying on a great tradition.' Then, having performed her public duty, like a lady opening a fête, she suddenly became her usual self and dashed up to the children to beg a reward.

Podge was too excited to eat his biscuit. He felt tremendously important and somehow satisfied, as if he had at last done something he was meant to, or at least begun to do the things that a real grown-up terrier should. It was a Big Day.

3

Sir Charles

In which Podge is shown round the Estate and meets a very distinguished personage

ODGE slept well that night, dreaming of a succession of rats which he had to fight. They were all enormous and immensely strong, with glaring hypnotizing eyes and long thick evil tails. They rose up before him one after another, each more gigantic and horrid than the last, and with calm efficiency he disposed of them all. He dreamed that Minnie and Manager were praising him and saying how pleased They would be, and he heard the expressions of amazement and delight from the farmer and his wife as they too watched him triumph. He grunted with satisfaction.

In his sleep his paws twitched and he barked faintly. Minnie and Manager sat talking beside him in the straw,

looking at him from time to time with amusement and a sort of pride.

'Well, I always thought he'd turn out to be a useful kind of puppy—useful, that's what,' said Manager. Minnie knew very well that at first he had not welcomed the idea of having to bring up a puppy at all, and that later on he had said Podge was too fat and too slow to be any use; but being in her own way a tactful dog she didn't say anything.

'I always say that breeding will tell,' she agreed, 'And you must admit that the Family always were ones for ratting. Now, I think he mightn't make too tall for going to Earth—and then he'd have a Career in front of him. I well remember his father, old Matchbox, now. A great dog he was when he was young: he was that quick on his feet, and once he got down he'd never budge, no matter what he had in front of him. They tell me that Podge's brother, Mark, looks to be a good puppy, too. I remember when I was a puppy up there . . .'

Manager found this family reminiscence boring, and he resented the way Minnie kept reminding him of her aristocratic connections. (Though he was of the same breed, his family had been farm dogs for several genera- tions, whereas Minnie had been born and brought up at the Great House.) He scratched at a flea rather pointedly, and said:

'Yes . . . Well, I've been thinking, now, Minnie, that since the puppy's done so well today it might be time enough to show him round. I'm pleased with him, very pleased. He's big enough to hunt on his own now, I'm thinking, so the sooner he knows where everything is the better. In fact, since there's a good moon tonight we might as well begin at once. No time like the present, I always say.'

Minnie agreed. She always enjoyed hunting, especially at night, and tonight was lovely and clear, with a bright moon and fluffy white clouds standing out rather sharply from the very dark sky. It was fairly still, with only a small breeze. She could visualize the fields stretching down to the stream at the bottom of the valley and then rising up on the other side to the wood surrounding the Great House; and in her mind she checked over the holes she knew and the places that were good for rabbits. Taking the puppy on a conducted tour would give her a good excuse to visit them all—perhaps more briefly than she would have liked, but still, it was the first time since Podge had come that she would have time to do them all, instead of dashing back to make sure he hadn't woken up and missed her.

She went over to wake Podge, shaking him gently. He snarled and jerked his head round, baring his teeth as if to bite her—his instinctive defence while he was still three-quarters asleep—but almost immediately realized that it was her and coughed apologetically.

'Sorry,' he said. 'Wasn't really awake.'

'Ne'mind,' said Minnie. 'Sorry to wake you, but we felt, Manager and I, that it was time you had a look round the Estate. Huntin' an' all that, don't you know.'

Podge had noticed how she always spoke in a different way whenever she was talking about hunting or the Family, or the Great House: somehow she became more dignified and more anxious to make an impression. It was almost as if she were acting a part, and yet it was as much a real version of herself as her everyday speech and manner, when she talked dialect and was gossipy and easy-going. At this moment her 'official' self was on top, as it had been when he caught the rat.

'The time has come,' she continued, 'For you to begin huntin' on your own. You have proved your worth. We will show you the best places.'

Manager waited with a kind of bored tolerance. Then 'Come on,' he said, and the three of them left the barn and crossed the moonlit yard.

Podge had never been farther than the gate at night. Everything had a strange resemblance to its day-time self; things looked somehow larger and flatter, as though they had had cardboard replicas put in their places; distance was very difficult to judge, for everything seemed closer than it had been by day; colours were simplified—everything was in tones of green or silvery-grey. It was all rather strange, slightly frightening, and very beautiful.

They trotted down the lane, finding their way sure-footedly over the rough, slippery stones, which the tractors and lorries had polished smooth once the mud dried and shrank in the summer heat. Overhead the tall elm trees were thickly leaved, just beginning to change colour. Birds flapped, startled, from the branches as they went by; pigeons flew away, their wings making a strange whistling sound; an owl hooted from the roof of the old empty cottage down the lane; in the field a cow rose jerkily to her feet and suspiciously watched them pass, her horns lowered.

They reached the bottom of the lane, where it branched, the left fork leading to the village and the right up to the fields. Here the mud was thicker, dried now into deep ruts, and the elm trees continued, a row on either side, making the boundary between the lane and the fields. Opposite the dogs was a gate leading into a field which stretched down to the stream at the bottom. Under this they crawled, and cantered down the winding path which the cows had made for themselves as they came to and fro for milking. They went in single file: Minnie leading, then Podge, then Manager solemnly bringing up the rear.

At the bottom a bridge spanned the stream, and beyond was a rough hummocky field going steeply uphill, with a crown of trees at the top. They crossed over, skirted the marshy patch the other side and cut across the field to the far hedgerow, which was thickly overgrown with brambles and nettles and studded with trees.

Minnie dived into the hedge through a gap between two brambles. Podge followed rather doubtfully. Under the thick tangle, which from the outside had looked quite impenetrable, there was in fact a series of little tracks, branching and dividing and winding in and out of the undergrowth, over and around and beneath the roots of the trees. These tracks led to various holes. Some belonged to rabbits; and the older dogs showed Podge how to tell by the smell whether the rabbit was in or not. Two were larger, and smelt quite differently—a very strong smell. These were the two entrances to a fox-hole or Earth. The fox was out, probably hunting or visiting other foxes in the Big Wood around the Great House. Minnie warned Podge that foxes were to be avoided until he was fully grown, and never in any circumstances to be attacked in the open—at least, not by a terrier.

'Our job,' she said proudly, 'is to go and attack them in the Earth; and once you've caught hold of them you must *not let go*. This is a job that only we can do. It is the hounds' job to chase them above ground and to catch them there. Perhaps you may see them one day if you're lucky.'

Podge made a resolution he would not only do that but he would one day go down an Earth and bravely attack the fox there; and he would *not let go*; but he didn't say this to Minnie or Manager.

After they had fully inspected this heggerow, working their way along it, they emerged at the top end on the crest of the hill. They followed the hedge along the top of the field, at right-angles to the rabbit-hedge, and after a while came steeply downhill to a gate, under which they crawled. The field they were now in stretched up to the very edge of the Big Wood itself. It was an impressive sight. The trees were very tall and thick, and by night rather black. It seemed enormous. To their left as they faced it, it went along the length of the field up to the drive of the Great House; to the right it came to a right-angled corner, and then went away almost straight for as far as they could see, with the fields marching along the side of it.

'This is the Big Wood,' said Minnie impressively. Podge *was* impressed. He had never seen any single thing so big. As they came up the hill to the edge of the wood he could begin to see a little way into the shadows beneath the first trees at the edge, where there was a fairly thick undergrowth of bracken and leaves and brambles and ferns. And as they got closer, too, he realized that the wood was not silent as it had seemed from a distance: it was full of night noises—rustlings in the undergrowth, movements in the trees, the odd call of a startled bird, and nearer at hand and very frightening indeed, a sudden sharp unknown bark which sent a tingle along his spine and made his hackles rise.

They had been skirting the wood, running down a little shallow ditch beside a steep bank on their left which marked the edge of the wood. The ditch was dry at this time of the year, and its smooth bed, free of brambles and twigs or old leaves, showed that it was much used as a pathway by the inhabitants of the wood. They kept silent, following the path of the ditch to the edge of the next field, where it went under the hedge and joined a small stream. There was water in this, running quite quickly over its stony bed to the right where at the bottom of the valley it joined the main brook that they had crossed at the very beginning of their journey. They turned left, however, and followed the stream up on the other side of the hedge towards the wood.

'Never does to go very far into the Big Wood,' said Manager. 'Can never be sure who you'll meet. They don't like to be disturbed. Lots of things goin' on here— busy, y'know. Foxes, 'n pheasants, 'n shootin' 'n log-cuttin'. It's not strictly our territory, except this first bit here, up to the path.'

The path was actually quite close, and ran along parallel to the edge of the wood. Their stream came from a little artificial lake just the other side of the path, but the

water was clear and fresh, and the lake was obviously filled by a spring.

'Some likes swimmin',' said Manager with a grin, indicating the lake. 'Can't say I care for it myself.' They turned right and followed the path, which was grassy and bordered by very tall trees, mostly dark pines and firs though there were still one or two elms here as well. Their paws made no sound in the thick wet grass. Suddenly as they came round a slight corner they surprised a rabbit which fled away to the left among the trees, with Podge rocketing after it and crashing through the thick undergrowth. The older dogs stopped, looking dubiously at each other.

'Silly idiot,' said Manager, with just a shade of anxiety as well as annoyance in his voice. 'Hope he don't meet Anyone. Don't take very kindly to trespassers, they don't.' They watched Podge's dim white shape getting farther away and fainter in the darkness.

'I'd better go,' said Minnie. 'Wait here and watch out, will you? Let me know if Anyone comes.'

Podge had realized by this time that he wasn't going to catch the rabbit, which had had a head start and anyway knew the wood inside out. He stopped, feeling rather foolish and thinking that he had better go back. He turned, and began picking his way back through the bracken, following the path which he himself had trampled. Just at this moment he became aware of a pair of green eyes in front of him, regarding him steadily and with some malice. He stopped abruptly. He had heard nothing.

'Well,' said a rasping voice. 'And what do you think you're doin'? Nasty things can happen to those who trespass. Not really done, is it, to go crashin' through other people's territory scarin' the things they're carefully huntin'? *I* shan't get my supper tonight—though I don't suppose that bothers you, does it, eh?'

The eyes came a little closer, glowing very brightly and not blinking at all, staring straight at Podge. Struck with a sudden terrible fear, and feeling very small indeed, Podge found himself cringing and shrinking to the ground. He couldn't manage to say anything. Somehow he knew exactly what sort of animal this was, and the knowledge didn't help at all. He could hear the faint swish of the fox's brush, and he could sense its whiskers twitching. It came closer, moving quite soundlessly over the dry bracken.

Suddenly it gave a short, gruff laugh.

'Well, well, a puppy!' it said. 'That explains it. Never been up here before, eh? Sorry if I scared you—always like that when I'm huntin'—too many people dashin' round spoilin' the game—makes me livid. You'll know better in future, no doubt. Know the way back? Who're you with? Anyone I know?' He paused, having, it appeared, run out of breath and questions; and with relief Podge stammered:

'Minnie and Manager.'

'Oh, yes,' replied the fox noncommittally. 'We've met.'

At this point Minnie emerged rather tentatively from the shadows where she had been hiding. The fox showed no surprise—he had of course seen her coming. They regarded each other with elaborate but strained courtesy.

'Evenin', she said. 'Sorry an' all that. Rather green, don't you know.' (This referred to Podge, though he didn't understand it—which was perhaps as well—and meant both young and inexperienced.)

'Quite so, quite so,' said the fox politely. 'Don't mention it . . . No doubt you'll be wantin' to potter off— mustn't take up your time, y'know . . . Er, fine evenin',' he added as an afterthought, 'Especially for the time of year.'

'Indeed,' said Minnie. 'Don't let us keep you, however. You must be very busy.'

'About the same as usual. Mustn't grumble,' replied the fox. 'Charmin' puppy you have there. I expect we shall be seein' more of him. From the Great House, is he, eh? Chip off the old block! Well, a very good evenin' to you.' He turned to go, his nose twitching with suppressed indignation, then added over his shoulder:

'Oh, and by the way, do let me know if ever you're comin' this way again, won't you. Be delighted to see you, of course.'

They parted with obvious relief. He melted into the darkness as silently as he had come, carrying his fine brush like a banner. Minnie shook herself as if to get rid of something unpleasant and uncomfortably unpredictable.

'I hope you realize just how awkward a situation you got us into,' she observed, growling. Podge had indeed noticed how thin was the layer of politeness the fox and dog maintained, and how each remark carried a double meaning. He admired Minnie's courage in coming out to talk with the fox and to defend him, and he felt that in many ways they had seemed very alike. In a way he rather admired the fox, too. He had seemed such a splendid creature.

Minnie led the way back to the path where Manager waited, tense and alert.

'Met Sir Charles,' she explained briefly. 'Lovely manners all round.'

Manager chuckled:

'First time lucky,' he observed.

They followed the path up to a gate leading out into the fields, and from there cut down to the stream again, investigating a couple of rabbit-patches on the way. Then they went along the stream towards home, sometimes walking along in the water where it was shallow, and at others scrambling up onto the banks and dodging through the young hazel thickets which grew there and which came right up to the water's edge, their branches arching over the water and making almost a tunnel, hidden from outside view. There were all sorts of interesting holes along here, some of them very big and deep, and Podge dutifully listened and memorized what the older dogs told him about them. But somehow it didn't seem very exciting after his adventure in the wood; and he didn't try any more hunting on his own, either!

Eventually they worked their way down to the first bridge again. There they left the water, and made their way back up the fields to the farm and sleep, feeling tired but satisfied.

4

Podge Left out

In which Minnie and Manager are unusually secretive and Podge eventually learns the reason

ODGE woke up the next morning with a feeling of excitement. For a moment he didn't know what had made him feel like this, and then he remembered the adventure of the night before, and how they had met the dangerous and attractive Sir Charles in the Big Wood. He was a little disappointed that Minnie and Manager didn't share his excitement: they were, indeed, rather abrupt with him, for they were busy talking about something he didn't understand; they hardly listened when he tried to remind them. So he went off and tried telling his adventure to the pigs, but they only grunted and rolled over onto the other side to catch the sun; and to the cows, but they only mooed and went on eating grass, for that was all they cared about. Finally he went to the horses; they stamped their feet and pricked their ears attentively.

'Ah, we know him,' said Silver Queen, swishing her long thick grey tail. 'Sometimes we've come across him when we've been out for a ride in the fields, lurking at the edge of the wood with a pheasant in his jaws; once he came up here trying to steal our chickens, but we heard him and whinneyed and neighed and galloped round until He came out to see what was the matter, then Sir Charles went away; and once we hunted him.'

'Tell me about Hunting,' said Podge.

'It's the most exciting thing there is,' replied Perriwinkle, the brown horse who shared the field with Silver Queen. 'You get up in the morning, knowing that something exciting is going to happen, and you're groomed till you shine' (at this he looked with pride at his dark coat, which shone like a polished conker). 'And then you go in a box to the Meet, where you see all your friends and have a chat with them before it starts. And there are three of us with riders in red coats; and the hounds are there, all eager and excited. Then the huntsman blows a horn, which is the most thrilling sound there is and which sends shivers right through you, so that you want to gallop off at once; and you dance and fidget and though your rider tells you to stop you can feel that he wants to gallop off too. Then you follow the hounds and the riders in red to a wood, and you wait there until it becomes almost unbearable. At last you hear the hounds shouting out that they've found the scent of a fox, and they dash off after it; and *then* you can gallop. You try to keep as close to the hounds as you can, and all around you your friends are galloping with their heads down, pulling like trains. Your rider leans forward and urges you on, and you jump enormous fences and ditches and and and—oh well, it's marvellous.'

His eyes were shining and he was standing very upright and alert. Silver Queen sighed deeply.

'Yes, it's just like that,' she said, 'Only better, of course. And you're *so* tired when you get home, though

all day you've felt as though you could go on galloping for ever.' They fell silent, dreaming about the hunts they had had, forgetting Podge and his questions. He looked at them with wonder, almost envying them. What fun they had had. He wished he too could take part in this glamorous and thrilling thing. He had sensed the glamour of it meeting Sir Charles, and now he felt even more strongly how wonderful it must be.

He pottered slowly back across the yard and lay down by the milk-stand, thinking, until some time later the farmer called him to help bring the cows in. Somehow the everyday life of the farm seemed a little tame compared with these things he had heard about. In fact once he had finished helping with the cows and had failed to find either Minnie or Manager anywhere, he felt rather bored.

He waited crossly for them to return, passing the time by chasing the calves, who didn't really want to play and whose mothers became angry with him. Minnie and

Manager didn't help matters when they did come back by refusing to tell him where they had been—though he had a shrewd guess that they had been collecting news and gossip from their friend Flossie at the Lodge—and by appearing surprised to find him still there. They soon became very busy making a large new straw bed at the back of the barn, but they didn't explain who or what it was for.

'Ah, it's a secret,' they said.

In fact, they ignored Podge altogether. He almost got the impression that they were waiting for him to start doing things on his own, now that he had proved he was old enough. This went on for several days. The older dogs went off together each morning, leaving Podge by himself. He helped the farmer a bit now and then, but there was really very little to do; the children went back to school, and he had no-one to play with him. Eventually he said to himself:

'All right, I *will* go off and hunt on my own, just to show them.' Having said this, he felt much better, and slipped out of the yard and trotted off down the lane. At the bottom he turned left, exploring new ground. He felt very independent.

He soon came to an old empty cottage on his right, and decided to go in and have a look round the garden. He crawled under the gate and found himself in a yard, rather smaller than that at the farm, which joined on to the side of the house. It had once been gravelled, but now it was overgrown with weeds. There was a rusty pump up against the wall, some rough grass at the bottom end of the yard, with a tumbledown fence separating the garden from the field behind. He went through an open gateway at the corner of the house to the back. Here there was a terrace, and beyond it grass again, which had grown very long during the summer. But the back door of the house was open and through it he could see men working inside. The cottage wasn't going to be empty much longer, it seemed.

'Now I shall have some news for Minnie and Manager,' he thought. 'I wonder who will come here.'

He stood for a moment looking at the house, then made his way through the long grass to the inviting-looking field beyond. As he had hoped, the grass was short and cropped close, and he could smell rabbits. Quietly he padded over the grass towards a large patch of brambles at the foot of an old apple-tree. This seemed a likely spot to find rabbits. He came up to the patch and began sniffing. He could smell rabbit very clearly inside, but he didn't know which way it would try to escape. Unfortunately, while he was thinking about it, wondering what best to do, his nose began to tickle and he simply had to sneeze. The rabbit promptly bolted—the other side—and though he ran after it he was too slow to catch it.

Disappointed, he returned to the brambles. Everything it seemed had gone wrong these last few days, apart from the wonderful stories of the hunt. He felt bored, with nothing much to do on the farm. He didn't feel that he was really needed. Two dogs were quite enough to do all that the farmer wanted dogs for, and though they let him help it was, he felt, only as a kindness. He felt rather lonely again, for now that he had proved he could do things that a grown-up terrier could Minnie and Manager seemed to have left him alone.

In fact, of course, they had done this deliberately, for

they felt that now that Podge had learnt to catch rats and
had been shown how to hunt he should learn to do these
things without them there to help. All terriers are by
nature independent dogs: even though they like company
very much and enjoy doing things in groups, they need
to be quite capable of hunting alone, for the work for

which working terriers have been bred is essentially a
lonely job. Only one terrier can go down one hole at a
time, and even when an Earth is big and has several ways
in, so that more than one dog is used, only one can
actually face the fox. That demands great courage, and
this sort of courage comes partly through having done
things on your own.

While Podge was sitting by the brambles feeling rather
miserable, he heard the sound of an enormous lorry
coming slowly up the lane. Its engine sounded different
from those of any of the cars or lorries which came
regularly to the farm. Curious, and excited at something
different happening, he hurried through the garden out

into the lane, and then up to the farm as fast as his legs could carry him.

And there he found something which explained Minnie and Manager's odd behaviour, why they had been so anxious to collect gossip from Flossie, and why they had been so busy making the new straw bed. The lorry stood in the middle of the yard, and near it stood the farmer and his wife, and a strange man whom Podge immediately recognized as a friend to dogs. Over his ordinary clothes he wore a knee-length brown kennel-coat. His face was brown and wrinkled, weather-beaten by being outdoors a lot. He had a kind smell.

In his arms he was holding two dogs, a little larger than Minnie, though with thinner bones, who all the same

were quite obviously puppies. They had soft skin, which seemed about two sizes too large, enormous paws, long, floppy ears, long pointed faces with soft and rather droopy jowls, and long tails. They were mainly white, with a few small patches in brown and rusty black. They looked very miserable.

Minnie and Manager stood at the feet of the strange man, looking up at him with adoration. They called Podge:

'Look,' they said. 'Hound puppies. We didn't tell you—wanted it to be a surprise. You must help us look after them and teach them things. You're just the right age for them.'

Podge suddenly felt that everything was right again, and that it had all been worth it. Now he had something he could do, and companions nearer his own age, who could play with him and be silly sometimes where Minnie and Manager were too old.

'Who's the Friend?' he asked. Minnie and Manager understood immediately. 'Oh, he's Ken, the Huntsman,' said Minnie. 'He's brought us these puppies from the Pack to look after till they're old enough to hunt.'

Ken, who had been busy talking when Podge joined them, suddenly noticed him.

'Oh, that's the puppy, is it?' he said. 'Well, he's a good 'un. Come along then Magpie, my beauty, there's a good dog.'

Podge bounced up and down with delight and excitement, ready to do anything Ken asked. He had such a friendly, rather gruff voice, which sounded as if it was always obeyed, but from love not fear.

'Make a good terrier, that,' Ken continued. 'Nice little dog. Not too leggy. Just like his father. How old is he? Seven months, eh? Next season, then p'raps. Well, I'll give you these and then I'd best be getting along. Give him someone to play with—and teach him a bit, I'll be bound.' He gave a short chuckle. 'Do that puppy good to have to nurse these for a bit,' he said. 'Give him a sense of responsibility.' He and the farmer both laughed.

He tickled Podge behind the ears and thumped him on the back. Then he patted Minnie and Manager too, shook hands with the farmer and climbed back into his brown lorry. He drove out of the yard and off down the lane with a final wave.

The two hound puppies sat in the middle of the yard and howled.

5

New Friends

In which Doctor and Dorothy introduce themselves

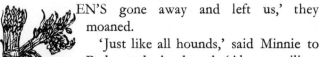

'EN'S gone away and left us,' they moaned.

'Just like all hounds,' said Minnie to Podge under her breath. 'Always wailing, especially when they're young. Never keep quiet about anything, they don't. Not like terriers, now.' But aloud she said, 'Now then, don't you fret. You'll see Ken again when you're a bit bigger, and we'll look after you. We've made you a nice bed all ready, and there's some milk and meal waiting for you.'

The bigger hound, who was a dog, and who had black and dark brown markings on his head, back and right side, stopped howling and looked more cheerful:

'Dinner?' he said, 'Gosh, I *am* hungry.'

His sister still howled, but less noisily. The farmer picked them up, one under each arm, and took them across to the barn, the other dogs following him. There he put them down beside their bowl of meal, patted them, and then went back to his work.

The hound puppies started eating. Even the bitch found that hunger was stronger than misery, and began to eat. She was mostly white, with faint brownish markings on her head and right side, and blackish ones along her left side. She was like her brother, but much lighter and more delicate in every way. Podge watched them eating with absolute fascination: he had never seen food disappear so fast. If he had known what a vacuum-cleaner was he would have recognized the likeness between it and the hounds. The three terriers stood round watching, feeling a little superior and very affectionate towards the puppies: they were so lovable. Podge felt that life had suddenly become very exciting and full of all sorts of possibilities.

'Now then,' said Minnie when the puppies had finished, 'Introductions. I'm Minnie; this is Manager; and this is Podge. Who're you?'

The puppies looked at her with enormous brown unblinking eyes, fringed absurdly with delicate white eyelashes. The bitch spoke, rather shyly:

'This is Doctor,' she said, 'and I'm Dorothy.'

'That's fine,' said Minnie. 'I expect you'll be wanting to see where you sleep. Your bed's here, behind these bales. We sleep farther forward, nearer the yard, so we can hear if anything comes.'

Dorothy went to inspect the bed, and came back graciously waving her long fine tail. 'That's splendid,' she said. 'How kind of you.'

Podge admired her for her calmness and for a certain queenliness she had. It was difficult to believe that only a few minutes ago she had been howling and making a fuss, miserable and very puppyish. Now she was quite in command of herself and very royal and dignified. Doctor, on the other hand, was quite hopelessly undignified. He lay there sprawled out, legs everywhere and his broad blunt nose stretched flat on the straw. He didn't seem in the least graceful, as his sister was; but he was very friendly and was soon telling Podge all about the Kennels where they had been born and where they had lived until this morning. Podge lay beside him, leaning up against Doctor's great side, listening intently to every word.

'Oh, it's a grand place,' Doctor said. 'There are *ever* so many of us there—I couldn't count them. Some of them are very old and covered with scars from all the times they've been hunting, and from fighting to keep their places as Head Dogs in the kennels. At night you can hear them telling the others all about the wonderful runs they've had and the foxes they've caught, and the things they did when they were young. They're very big and fierce, and it doesn't do to go too close to them.'

'How big?' interrupted Podge, who had never seen a dog bigger than Manager.

'About four times as big as me, some of them,' said Doctor, then added cautiously, 'Well, nearly.'

'Oh,' said Podge weakly, failing to imagine how a dog could be as big as Doctor suggested. There seemed to be so *much* of Doctor in all directions already, and he was only a puppy. 'Will you get to be as big as that?'

'I expect so,' said Doctor nonchalantly, 'Most of us do, y'know.'

Podge shut his eyes. He supposed he would get used to the idea in time—and it would be rather fun to have two such huge and beautiful dogs for his friends.

Doctor went on telling him about the Kennels. He said that the older dogs were kept in large rooms, bitches in one and dogs in another, where they had benches to lie

on, and that outside there were large yards where they went during the day. Then there were bigger yards still, where they were exercised, and fields too, all round the Kennels. There was a big stable yard where the horses were kept, and houses where Ken and his Whipper-in, Jack, and all the grooms and other people lived. There was always lots going on—many people coming and going, and the noises of hounds, horses and people all working and talking and joking and arguing and gossiping all day.

'Of course, we had a room to ourselves,' Doctor said, 'with our mother and brothers and sisters (there were five of us). But we heard and saw most of what was going on.'

Podge liked the sound of the Kennels, and he was sure that anywhere where Ken was would be happy and fun to be. But he didn't like the idea of being shut in so much of the time, of being with so many other dogs always, of not being free to come and go just when and where he chose. But then, he was a terrier, not a hound.

He was surprised at how grown-up the hound puppies were, in their different ways—much more so than he had been at their age. And he found during the next few days and weeks that they had already got the idea of hunting. They spent their first full day at the farm exploring, going into every building, examining every corner, their noses on the ground sniffing all the time. They seemed to find out such a lot more by smelling than Podge did, and they were much more inquisitive than he had been. They wanted to know about everything: what things were, where they came from, what they were for, and why why why all the time. Podge found by the end of the day that he was very tired, his paws ached from trotting after them, for his legs were much shorter than theirs and he had to hurry to keep up with them, and his head buzzed with all the things he had had to try to tell them. But he was terribly pleased that they had come, and rather proud that he was able to explain things to them as Manager and Minnie had done to him.

All day Doctor and Dorothy had been bouncy and full of energy and excitement and curiosity; but when the evening came and all the dogs went into the barn to sleep they suddenly remembered that they were a long way from home and from their friends and family. They missed the familiar noises of people and horses clumping around, and the farm seemed very silent indeed, with only the sounds of owls and winds instead of the older hounds talking as they lay on their benches. And though the farmer was kind when he came to see if they were all right, he wasn't Ken doing his rounds before shutting up and going to bed. They lay side by side in their straw bed, put their noses down to their big paws and whimpered.

Podge heard them, and after a moment he felt he couldn't let them go on being unhappy by themselves. So he got up and went across to them, rather diffidently.

'Please don't be sad,' he said. 'I know you miss the Kennels; but you'll be going back there when you're old enough to hunt, and everyone will still be there and very pleased to see you. Think how horrid it would be being there now and not being old enough to hunt, and having to wait and do nothing while all the others went out. There are lots of good places to hunt here, and lots of big holes—and *lots* of foxes. I know, I've met one.'

Up till now Doctor and Dorothy had been listening without much attention; but at this they lifted their heads and looked at Podge eagerly.

'How lucky you are!' said Doctor. 'Was it big? Was it *fierce*?'

'*Tell* us about it,' commanded Dorothy. They made a space for Podge between them, and he lay down and told them all about his meeting with Sir Charles—though he didn't feel he really needed to tell them quite how frightened he had been.

By the time he had finished they were feeling much better; and though they were still missing the Kennels very much they had decided that coming to the farm wasn't perhaps such a very bad thing after all, and that it might help them to be good at hunting later on. The hounds and Podge curled up together in the warm hollow behind the bales, and went peacefully to sleep,

while the two older dogs sat in their usual positions at the front of the barn.

'What did I tell you?' said Minnie with satisfaction. 'I always said that what that puppy needed was others nearer his own age—do him good to nurse 'em a bit. Give him a sense of responsibility, I said.'

Being in his own way a tactful dog, Manager didn't remind her that that was what Ken had said the day before. He only grinned to himself. 'They'll do,' he said.

6

New People

In which an important discovery is made

N the days and weeks that followed Podge and the two hound puppies became almost inseparable. They did everything together. Podge took them round 'the Estate', as he had been taken by Minnie and Manager; and together they explored all the fields, the hedgerows and streams near the farm. They never went farther into the village than the old cottage, where the workmen were still busy—although they always had time to pat the puppies and play with them for a while—but they went right up into the Big Wood by day, exploring all the big rides cut through it and the little tracks through the undergrowth as well; and they also explored farther on to the right of the farm, where the fields climbed a little higher and turned into big open downy country, and where instead of cattle there were cornfields—cut now, of course, with only their stubble remaining—and sudden ridges with wide and beautiful views. It was farther than Minnie or Manager would ever have bothered to go: their interests were centred on the farm and the village and what went on there; but the hounds were adventurous and liked wandering, and so Podge grew to like it too.

They would scent out the interesting trails, using their sensitive noses, and Podge would in his turn investigate the holes which Doctor and Dorothy were rapidly becoming too large to go down.

They grew at an enormous rate, and soon left Podge far behind. He was not far from his full size now, as the autumn wore on. The nights began to get colder, and the dogs were glad of each other's warmth as they huddled together in the straw. The leaves started falling, and hunting became much more fun, since it was easier for them to make their way through the bushes and brambles and woods, and the scents stayed longer and more clearly in the mornings on the ground made hard by frost.

It was about this time of year that something rather exciting happened, which gave Podge and his friends a new interest and which was to be an important event in Podge's life, though he didn't realize it at the time. One morning Podge and the hounds decided they would go hunting for rabbits in the fields down by the village. As soon as they could decently get away from the farm after helping bring the cows in, they ran off down the lane, their breath coming in white clouds, for there had been a frost during the night, though now the sun was just beginning to come out.

At the bottom of the lane they paused, and had a surprise. The old empty cottage wasn't empty any more. The windows were open and they could hear noises from inside. In the yard there was an enormous van. People were rushing from the van to the house carrying pieces of furniture, and from the house to the van again to fetch more, issuing instructions all the time:

'That goes in the sitting room.'

'I think we'd better put that packing case in here for the moment.'

'Watch that corner, Joe.'

'Where shall I put this, Miss?'

'Would you like some tea? We're having some.'

'Oho, new people,' said Podge.

'This looks fun,' said Dorothy.

'Come on,' said Doctor, ambling ahead. They entered the yard in procession—Doctor first, being the biggest, then Dorothy, and Podge trotting importantly in the rear, his black ears cocked and his stumpy tail vibrating gently, ready to wag at any moment. They caused something of a diversion. The removal men, who had by now made themselves comfortable with their tea on a couple of packing cases in the middle of the yard, looking rather shipwrecked, were divided between trying to find somewhere to put their cups so that they could pat the dogs and being prepared if necessary to repel attack.

'Cor, proper hounds they are, Joe,' said one. 'Ever seen anything like 'em before?'

'And a tough little tyke with them, too,' said the other.

The hounds stood still with great dignity at these remarks; but Podge went to the side-door, which was open, to investigate.

Inside he saw a stone-floored room filled with jumbled things: wellington boots, mackintoshes, brooms, brushes, tins of polish, shopping-baskets, a riding hat, several packing cases filled with other tins and boxes. It led through into a kitchen, where three people were sitting amidst various pieces of furniture which looked as if they didn't belong there, drinking tea. Beyond this room again he could see another, the floor of which was covered with piles of books. He went to the step in the kitchen doorway, and stood there wagging his tail.

48

'Look, here's a dog come to visit us!' said the man. 'A terrier. Come on, old boy! Here!' His wife and daughter looked round, and made welcoming sounds. Soon Podge was being patted and loved and fed biscuits by them all.

He completely forgot about the hounds in his delight at finding three new friends. In a few minutes he heard indignant noises outside the back door:

'Disgraceful,' said Doctor's deep, lazy voice. 'Fancy leavin' us outside an' makin' friends without us.'

'You might at least introduce us,' said Dorothy severely. They both came through the open door with great dignity and stood on the step.

'Sorry,' puffed Podge through a mouthful of biscuit. 'Nice people. Come an' see.'

'Oh, *hounds*!' said the girl, getting up. 'Super hound puppies. Hul*lo* then!'

At the friendly sound of her voice the hounds immediately lost all their pretended dignity and waved their tails furiously, jumping up at her and pushing each other in their eagerness to get the most attention, stuffing their noses and paws into her pockets. Then they went and introduced themselves to her father and mother. Podge stood in the middle, looking very proud and taking all the credit for having so cleverly found their new friends.

The family gave them all biscuits and tea in saucers (which they suspected at first but, having once tasted, consumed with delight and much splashing and licking each other's whiskers afterwards). They were again made a fuss of and then put firmly outside so that the family could get on with the unpacking.

'Come back later when we're not so busy,' they said. The three dogs were very pleased with these new friends.

'Must tell Minnie and Manager,' said Podge. 'Won't they be cross we've found them first!'

They were. Minnie hadn't even known that anyone was coming to the cottage at all, and was very annoyed that Flossie, her usual source of local information, had failed her.

'Still, what can you expect of a spaniel?' she said. 'No perseverance, that's what!' and she sniffed indignantly. Manager said very little, but the gleam in his eye showed that he was thinking of the cottage as a possible source of bones. Later, the two older dogs made a joint expedition to the cottage, and came back satisfied that the three puppies had shown quite good taste in accepting the new people.

'A Good Family,' was the way Minnie put it. 'Nothing pretentious, but *I* can tell.'

So the cottage became a regular calling place for all the farm dogs, and they were always welcome. Sometimes they would help the family with the gardening—Dorothy was particularly keen on this, and would follow whoever was digging along the flower bed, sitting on each bit as it was dug. Doctor preferred investigating the barn and stable for mice, or digging along the flowerbeds by the edge of the house to find their holes. Podge as a mark of friendship would bring any rabbits he managed to catch to the cottage, and eat them there. Minnie established her position on the flowerbed by the side door, where it

was always warm and sunny; and Manager used to take the lids off the dustbins and help keep them from getting full by searching through the contents for old bones or scraps of meat. In fact, they completely adopted the family. In return, they were always petted, occasionally fed scraps or biscuits, and often taken for walks or allowed to follow when the girl went out riding. Even the familiar fields became more interesting when they went with people instead of by themselves, even if they couldn't do so much hunting. They were all very glad that their new friends had come.

7

Night Rescue

In which Podge goes hunting and displays presence of mind

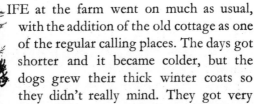IFE at the farm went on much as usual, with the addition of the old cottage as one of the regular calling places. The days got shorter and it became colder, but the dogs grew their thick winter coats so they didn't really mind. They got very dirty out hunting now, as the lane and fields were wet and muddy, and they spent long hours when it got dark sitting in the straw cleaning themselves carefully, getting all the mud and thorns and burrs out of their coats and from between their pads.

Then in midwinter the snow came. Neither Podge nor the hounds had ever seen snow, because they had not been born when it fell the winter before. They were very excited. Doctor thought it was something to fight, and spent ages bouncing across the yard trying to bite it and hit it with his paws as it fell. Dorothy found the drifts much more fun, and would plunge into them with enormous enjoyment, covering herself almost completely, and emerging with her nose, eye-lashes and whiskers all covered in snow. Then they would have three-cornered fights in it, scattering it in all directions as they chased each other, and rolling each other over and

over in it. Minnie and Manager watched them tolerantly, rather bored by this juvenile behaviour. They had already seen all the snow they wanted to.

But all the dogs enjoyed travelling on the trailer behind the tractor when the farmer took the hay out to his cows and scattered it for them in the fields, and they all loved going for walks with the girl from the cottage. She would wade through the snow in her big wellington

boots, even when it came over half-way up them, and the dogs would either run beside her where the surface of the snow had frozen hard and could support their light weight, or, where it was soft, follow in single file behind, jumping from one footprint to another. Sometimes when they thought the snow was hard enough for them to walk on top the hard crust would suddenly give way, and they would disappear into the soft drifts beneath, scrambling out shamefacedly and covered in melting snow. But they always enjoyed these expeditions, and came back warm and glowing.

After the snow there came a thaw, when for a while it was much warmer and the surface of the ground became soft and muddy. And then there came a week of stormy weather. At night there were high winds, and the dogs could hear them howling outside the barn, and the trees creaking. In the morning when they went out they would find old twigs and small branches scattered in the lane and fields, and sometimes even a whole tree which had become rotten inside and only needed high winds to uproot it and bring it down. The dogs used to enjoy helping the workmen saw up these trees and load the logs onto their huge lorries.

Minnie said that it was silly to go too far from the farm when the weather was like this—it wasn't safe, she said, especially at night or alone. And especially it wasn't safe to go near trees or the Big Wood—you never knew when a branch might suddenly drop down on you. But after a few days Podge got fed up with being near home all day, and decided to go off hunting when night came and the older dogs were asleep. When the time came he poked Doctor and said:

'What about going hunting, now?' but Doctor only grunted and replied:

'I'm sleepy. Go away!' and Dorothy only opened one eye and said:

'You must be mad. Only a terrier would think of it.' Then they both turned over and went to sleep again.

Podge was cross. He jolly well wasn't going to give up his hunting just because they were too lazy to come with him, he thought. He'd go alone; and wouldn't they be cross in the morning when they found what fun he'd had. So he went very quietly to the front of the barn, and managed to get out without waking the older dogs. (Manager always said that he never *really* slept—he always had one eye open all the time—but now he was not only asleep but snoring.)

Outside in the yard it was very dark, and the wind was strong. It was pouring with rain, which the wind blew towards him. It stung his head and front. Podge was a bit discouraged, and felt that perhaps it would really be more fun to stay behind in the warm straw, where the old stone walls sheltered them from the wind and rain. And he wasn't quite so sure any more that hunting was much fun by yourself. He hesitated for a moment; but then he thought how impressed the others would be in the morning when he told them about the fun he'd had, and how scornful they might be if he didn't go after all. So he went.

The wind blew hard in his face, using the lane as a funnel, and the rain ran in rivers over the slippery stones, so that his feet and tummy got thoroughly splashed and muddy. He got very tired battling on, so at the bottom he turned right instead of going straight on down to the stream, so that for a little he would be sheltered from the wind by the hedge on his left, and from the rain by

the thick trees above him. Because of this when he did eventually reach the stream it was quite high up, where it ran closer to the Big Wood. He went up the field to the edge of the wood searching for scents all the way. Here the trees kept off some of the rain, and the force of the wind was broken; but he was disappointed to find that even here the heavy rain had washed away most of the scents, and that no-one except himself seemed to be about. Not a faint rustle in the undergrowth, not even the protesting squawk of a bird. He was cold, wet, tired, bored, annoyed and even almost a little afraid. He decided to go home.

So he made his way along the edge of the wood in the direction of the farm, so that he would only have a little way to go in the open. When he had nearly reached the little artificial lake he suddenly smelt a more recent scent than any he had come across so far. It was the scent of a dog; but not one that he knew. He caught occasional whiffs of it, but even though it had been left only a few hours before, the rain had already drowned the line, and he couldn't really follow it. He sniffed around for a few moments, puzzled. It was then that he heard the barking.

It was very faint and yet it didn't seem very far away. Somehow it was strangely muffled, too, and because of the wind Podge couldn't decide just what direction it was coming from. As far as he could understand it, it was saying: 'Help, I'm stuck!' but sometimes he wasn't even sure of that.

He marked to himself the look of the tree near which he had been when he had first heard it, and then he cast round it in a widish circle, hoping that by doing this he would suddenly come on another bit of scent. But he didn't. He was sure that there must be a dog stuck some-where close by. For a moment he couldn't think what to do. Then he remembered Doctor and Dorothy, and how well they could smell things even when the scent was faint to him.

'That's it,' he thought. 'I'll go and get them. They will know where this dog is.' Then he barked out as loud as he could, 'All right. I've heard you. I'll get help,' and hoped that whoever it was would hear him. Then he went as fast as he could back to the farm, hardly noticing the rain any more, though his paws still slipped in the wet grass and stuck in the mud down by the stream, and all his coat was flattened into wet rats' tails.

Doctor and Dorothy weren't very pleased to be woken. 'What, you again?' grumbled Doctor, 'Oh, bother your

58

dratted hunting. Can't you go to sleep and leave me in peace?' And Dorothy pinned down her long ears with her paws so that she couldn't hear.

'Oh, don't be silly: this is serious,' said Podge. 'I need your help, so for goodness' sake *wake up*. There's a dog stuck somewhere in the wood and the scent's so bad I can't find where he is, so you *must* come and help me. Only you've got good enough noses.'

This was different, and the hounds got up and shook themselves, not grumbling any more. Then they hurried with Podge down the wet lane into the storm, and back the shortest way to the Big Wood. Podge showed them the place where he had heard the barking, and took them to where he had smelt the scent, and then stood still and waited.

They sniffed the scent closely for a few seconds, then began casting round the spot to try to pick up the line. After a few moments Dorothy gave tongue to call Doctor to her, and then they both followed the scent through the undergrowth, quite slowly and with their noses very close to the ground since it was so faint. Every so often they stopped for a moment and sniffed round one spot before they found the scent again; and whenever they found it they said so, loudly. The line took them deeper into the wood, and eventually they traced it to the base of a very old oak tree growing by the edge of a deep and sunken stream.

As they came towards the tree they heard the barking again, more clearly than Podge had heard it before. Whoever it was was saying, 'I can hear you. Come on. I'm here.' Podge barked out:

'All right. We're coming. We'll soon get you out,'

though really he hadn't any idea how they would manage it.

When they got close to the tree they could see that it was hollow, and beneath the roots there was a large hole. Podge went to the mouth of the hole and barked down it:

'Are you down here?'

'Yes,' said the voice, rather muffled. ''Nother hole in the bank—come down that way.'

'Come down?' said Podge to himself. Doctor and Dorothy heard him.

'Of course you must go down,' said Dorothy firmly. 'Then you can see why he's stuck and how we can get him out.'

Podge felt a bit scared. He had never gone down a hole on his own before: always he had followed Minnie or only stuck his nose just inside. But this hole sounded deep; and besides it was night, and the hole had already trapped one dog. However, he realized that it might very easily have been him who was stuck, and he thought how horrid it must feel; so together with the hounds he looked along the stream to find the hole in the bank that the dog had mentioned.

They soon found it, behind a big root and rather over-grown. He had to stand in the stream and ease his front half in, and then scrabble until he had got the rest of him inside. It smelt damp and musty, as though no-one had been down there for some time. It also smelt faintly of fox. Soon he began to see more clearly how the tunnel turned away from its entrance in the bank.

The other dog had heard him coming.

'Not far off now,' he said. 'Hole branches—take the left fork.'

Podge came to the junction and followed his instructions. The right fork, he could see, led up almost straight to the surface, a little way off. A dim light was coming down it. He followed the left tunnel round a corner, and there was the trapped dog.

He was another terrier: very neat and brown and white (although now he was covered with dust and mud) with an intelligent head and fine thin face. He looked very relieved to see Podge at last.

'Thank goodness you've come,' he said. 'Didn't think I'd ever get out. Stupid of me. Haven't been down here since I was a puppy—forgot I'd grown—of course I'm much too big for it now—it's very narrow just here—roots, y'know. I'm quite stuck.'

He was. The tunnel narrowed quite suddenly just where he was, and its roof was made up of the interwoven fibres of small roots, with one big root passing directly above his back. It was this which had trapped him. His head and front paws had gone under it, but his body had been too deep, and he was pinned down firmly by the big root. Around him there was dust and earth which he had scraped loose trying to get through. At the sides the tunnel fitted a little less tightly, and the earth here was not made hard by roots. This gave Podge an idea.

'How tight *are* you wedged?' he asked. 'I mean, do you think you could move at all if I loosened the earth at the sides? If you could somehow get onto your side instead of your tummy you'd be less tightly wedged under the root, and then perhaps you could back out.'

The other dog shifted slightly.

'Yes, perhaps I might be able to move round a little,' he said, 'But I certainly can't go forward or back as I am.'

'I'd better go and tell my friends,' said Podge, 'If you don't mind waiting a moment, that is,' he added politely. 'Just in case they can think of anything better.'

He backed up the hole to where it branched, then turned and went out to the bank-entrance. Here Dorothy and Doctor were anxiously waiting. He explained briefly, and as they couldn't think of anything else to do and were too big to come down and help him Podge returned alone to the other dog, leaving his friends to keep watch outside.

It was a weary job. He scrabbled and scratched and soon both he and the other dog were sneezing and blinking in the thick dust. It took him quite a long while to shift enough earth to make even a little difference, and when he had moved it he had to push it away behind him. His paws got very tired, and his eyes were blinking, and his head ached. The trapped dog, powerless to do anything for himself, encouraged Podge, and in between bursts of digging they talked.

Podge learnt that his name was Masters, that he came from the Great House, and that his job was going down holes to hunt foxes.

'Such a stupid thing to do, when it's my profession,' grumbled Masters. 'Should have known better. I shall never live it down at the Club. The others'll never let me forget it.' Podge in his turn told Masters about his home and his friends Doctor and Dorothy, and how they had found where he was. Masters was impressed.

'Good show, that,' he said. 'Shockin' scent tonight— even an old hound would have had trouble with it. Pretty good of these puppies, I must say.'

By this time Podge had managed to shift quite a lot of earth on both sides of Masters. At last he paused, panting.

'Try now,' he said. 'If you can't move we'll have to think of something else.'

Masters concentrated, and tried as hard as he could to twist round. For a moment both he and Podge thought he was too tightly wedged; but suddenly he began to move, just a little. Gradually he twisted round till he was lying on his side in the tunnel. Then for a moment he lay there exhausted.

'If you try to back out I can push you,' said Podge. 'At least we know that the tunnel's big enough farther back, since you came down that way.'

'All right,' replied Masters. 'Now, then, let's try. One, two, three, *heave*!'

They both heaved together, and with a jerk Masters

63

shot back from under the root into the deeper part of the tunnel behind it, leaving Podge flat on his nose.

'Thank goodness,' they both said, and sat there for a moment, suddenly realizing how very tired they both were.

Then Masters got to his feet, shook himself painfully, and began backing along the tunnel. Podge realized that he could no longer go back the way he had come, as there were now piles of earth blocking the way. He had to go on under the dreadful root. Luckily he wasn't quite fully grown yet, and in any case he was slightly smaller-built than Masters, who was long and leggy, and deep in the body. Masters watched him anxiously; but Podge just managed to get through. They made their way back to the surface, where they found Dorothy and Doctor, who greeted them with delighted barks and wavings of sterns. Podge made the introductions, and his friends licked Masters' sore back for him and smoothed the rough and torn hairs back into place. Apart from this he was quite all right.

He went with them part of the way back along the edge of the wood, and then turned to go back to the Great House.

'Good night to you all,' he said, 'And thank you. I won't forget this. If any of you are ever needing a friend,

remember me. Any time, any where. I'll come. And good huntin'.'

Then he disappeared among the trees, and Podge and his friends took their way back to the farm, very wet, very tired, but very satisfied.

8

Farewell

In which Ken returns and there is a parting

THE rest of the winter went by very quickly, what with helping on the farm, hunting and visiting their new friends at the cottage. Now that the hounds were bigger and stronger and Podge his full-grown size they went farther afield. Once they went away across the fields behind the farm as far as the next village, and after exploring it for some time with great enthusiasm and curiosity the local policeman saw them and, thinking they were lost, put them in the cells for the night while he tried to find out where they came from. Dorothy was most indignant at this:

'I tried to explain that we were only paying a visit and not lost at all,' she protested, 'but he didn't seem to

understand. Really, I sometimes wonder just how intelligent humans are.'

Doctor wasn't at all upset: he enjoyed being put in a large cell with some old rags for a comfortable bed, and being fed frequently with bread and milk (though he would have preferred bones); and Podge found the whole thing very exciting. He felt very important indeed being shown into this cell, and he thought that the large kind policeman who took them there and fed them and made such a fuss of them was a splendid fellow. He could imagine himself telling Minnie and Manager about this adventure, and how impressed they would be. In fact, he and Doctor were rather disappointed when the farmer came early next morning to collect them. So was Dorothy, though she pretended not to be.

Then the spring came, and things began to grow again. The fields and woods were green, and the dogs went for long walks with the people from the cottage. The streams filled with rushing water, and they showed the girl from the cottage what fun it was walking along in the water, hidden almost completely down in the hollow and arched over by a tunnel of thick trees, with clear cold water swirling past over their paws and boots, the bright pebbles underfoot, and primroses and violets growing thickly along the steep banks, right down to the water's edge.

Late in the spring, when it was almost turning into summer, something important happened. One morning the dogs were just finishing rounding up the cows for milking, and they were all gathered round the last cow of all, who didn't want to leave the lush grass and come into the dull stall to be milked. The three dogs and two

67

hounds arranged themselves round her in a semi-circle, barking and making little rushes towards her, snapping at her feet. She stood there with her hooves planted firmly and obstinately, her head lowered, swinging it round crossly at them whenever they came too close and resolutely refusing to budge. This went on for some minutes. At last she moved one step in the direction of the open gate, having decided that as things were it would really be more peaceful inside than out; and at this critical moment a brown lorry ground its way up the lane.

Dorothy heard it first.

'Ken,' she said.

All the other stopped, and looked round. It was Ken indeed. So they all ran as fast as they could, barking joyfully, across the field, under the gate and into the yard. leaving the last cow puzzled, but very relieved and delighted to be able to resume her interrupted breakfast.

Ken got out of the cabin, and was at once surrounded by the five dogs. He patted them all, and looked closely at Doctor and Dorothy, seeming pleased with what he saw.

Then the farmer came out from the milking-shed, wiping his hands on his white overall, and they shook hands.

'Well, there they are, then,' the farmer said. 'We shall be sorry to see them go, of course—we always are—but that's how life is, isn't it?'

Doctor and Dorothy were already poking their noses into Ken's pockets, searching for titbits.

'He'll miss 'em, I expect,' Ken said, looking at Podge. 'Won't you, old man?'

The farmer nodded, patting Podge. 'Yes,' he replied.

'They've become very good friends indeed, Ken—go everywhere together. More like a hound than a terrier now in his habits, he is. Off hunting all the time. Even dug out one of the Great House terriers that was stuck in an earth the other night—or so it seems. Anyway the puppy was covered in earth and very tired the next

morning, and I'm told the other dog was marked across his back as though something like a root had caught him.'

'Oh, ah.' said Ken. 'Clever little beggar, then.'

'Yes, he'll miss 'em all right,' continued the farmer. 'It's a good job he's found some new friends down at the old cottage there: they'll help take his mind off it, and after a bit I reckon he'll forget it.'

'Pity he's not hunting,' said Ken. 'He'd enjoy that. Do him good, really—keep him occupied. He's the sort that needs a job to do or he'll get lazy and stubborn—I know that family. Not much good as a farm dog—too much energy and not enough to do with it.'

'Well, I agree with you, Ken,' answered the farmer. 'I've been thinking, and I'm not too happy about him. I don't really feel that this is the right place for him, or the right life. Still, what can I do? I mean, he's not my dog.'

'Ah, well, I suppose I'd better get going,' said Ken. 'I've got six more farms to visit before lunch.'

'Well, I mustn't keep you then. Shall I help you with them into the lorry?'

Doctor and Dorothy now realized that they were going back to the Kennels. They were very sad at leaving the farmer, who had walked them, but even more at leaving Podge; and though Podge was glad that they were going to be able to hunt properly at last he simply couldn't imagine what life at the farm would be like without them.

The five dogs said their goodbyes.

'Don't forget us,' commanded Dorothy. 'We'll come and see you whenever we're hunting this way.'

'I don't want to go,' said Doctor gruffly. 'Couldn't Podge come with us? I know he's small, but he hunts well—really he does. And he's much better at going down holes than we could ever be.'

But Ken didn't understand him.

'Tell the girl at the cottage to bring you to watch us,' said Doctor.

'And say goodbye to them all for us,' added Dorothy.

'I will,' Podge promised.

Then it was time for them to go. Ken put them in the

back of the lorry, got into the cabin and drove off, waving goodbye to the farmer. Podge could hear Doctor howling as the lorry went down the lane. He ran after it, but it was going too fast and soon left him behind, disappearing round the corner. Podge felt suddenly very alone. He still had Minnie and Manager; but the hounds were his best friends.

He trotted miserably on down the lane, not really knowing or caring where he was going. He came to the gate of the old cottage, and automatically turned in to the yard. The door was shut, but when he barked outside it he heard footsteps coming to let him in; and he knew that he wasn't completely alone after all.

9

Cubbing

In which Podge observes his first hunt and attempts to be a hound

FTER the hounds had gone Podge remained miserable: he missed them very much. His walks were lonely without them charging ahead all the time, always eagerly following a new scent, racing across the fields with their sterns high, or trotting slowly with their noses to the ground, intent and serious; he missed their company and their warmth at night—his straw bed seemed bare and cold without them on either side of him; and he found the everyday life of the farm and the jobs he had to do boring without them to share in it. Everything had been fun before, when the three of them did it together. Now it seemed dull. Every day was like every other day. He had no-one to play with, except occasionally when Minnie condescended to become frivolous for a short while.

Podge became naughty with his friends gone and nothing much to do. Sometimes to annoy the farmer he would pretend to round up the chickens, though he knew quite well that they didn't need rounding up, and would chase them across the yard with a look of terrific importance on his face, as though he was being terribly useful. At other times he would look for mice in the middle of the garden, digging up the plants. Or he would bury his oldest and nastiest bones there. And he didn't always

come when the farmer called him but ran away instead, or dodged just out of the way. At other times when he wasn't wanted and the farmer was doing something difficult, Podge would hang around, getting in the way, looking eager to help. Then the farmer would tell him off, or Minnie would smack him or Manager growl.

Altogether it wasn't a very happy summer. He thought very often of his friends, being trained now and with Ken and their relations all the time. He would go down to the cottage and sit in the yard and sulk. Only when his friends came out and played with him, or took him for a walk, did he feel happy again and forget about the hounds, and then he was like a lamb, gambolling beside them on perfectly straight legs, his tail wagging furiously and his head in the air, his eyes gleaming, snorting with pleasure and excitement.

Very early one September morning Podge was sitting out in the yard. He had woken early and, feeling disinclined to help fetch in the cows, had slipped off down the lane while the farmer wasn't looking. No-one was up at the cottage when he got there, so he curled up by the barn door and went to sleep. He was woken by the sound of the back door opening, and looked up, startled, to see the girl emerging, wearing a thick jacket and her big wellington boots. She seemed surprised to see him.

'Oh, it's you, Podge,' she said. 'I didn't expect you here so early in the morning. I'd better take you with me, I suppose.'

Podge didn't understand what she was talking about, but he was pleased to see her and looking forward to going for a walk. He stood by the door, waiting impatiently, while she went back inside, fetched something from a shelf and came out again, closing the door behind her. What she did next surprised him. She bent down and fastened a leather collar round his neck, and then walked off, leading him by the chain attached. Podge had never had a collar on before. It felt very odd, though it wasn't at all tight. But whenever he went to rush forward or sideways after a scent or another dog, or whenever he lagged behind, it pulled on his neck and reminded him that he wasn't free. He didn't mind this—in fact he felt rather proud trotting down the lane with the girl on the other end: it was almost as if he was taking her, instead of the other way round.

They didn't go for their usual walk—up the lane into the fields—but down into the village, where Podge had never been allowed before. Not many people were about so early, and only one or two dogs came to their gates to see who it was. They said good morning politely to each other as they passed. It was very quiet, and quite cold, and the sun shone rather weakly on the old tiled roofs and mottled grey-brown stones.

They went along the main street for a little way, then turned off into a narrow little lane. They passed a few cottages and farm buildings, and soon they were out

among the fields again. Here the cattle were already browsing, and birds singing or calling out in alarm as they passed. The light wind rustled in the thick hedge-rows and scattered a few dry brown leaves. The girl hummed and took big leisurely strides. Podge trotted briskly beside her. He didn't know where they were going or what they were doing, but he was enjoying himself.

The lane forked and crossed over the little local railway. On the other side it became even narrower and the hedges higher and thicker. Deep yellow grasses grew beside them, with fluffy seed-heads tossing as the wind caught them, and there were tall and beautiful clumps of teazles. They went on for quite a long way, occasionally passing a gateway into the fields, getting farther down into the flat vale towards the river, where the fields were wet and green.

Presently the lane came to a corner, where it turned right round some farm buildings. Straight on, there was only a rough and overgrown track. Just beyond the farm on the same side was a wood, running right down to the lane. At the far corner of the wood the girl stopped, and leaned on a gate which led into a field by the side of the wood. Obviously she was waiting for something. But what?

Podge looked between the warped and weathered bars of the gate along the edge of the wood. The field was empty, and he could neither see nor hear anything. They waited for what seemed a long time. Podge began to get rather excited. When was it going to happen, whatever it was?

Then suddenly he heard voices, quite faintly but not very far off, and the noise of animals swooshing through the deep wet grass. He pricked his ears and listened intently. He knew that the girl had heard them too, and he could see that she was staring at the gate right in the very far corner of the field next to the wood. Then he recognised one of the voices: Ken's. This must be hunting. He waited to see them come through the gate, terribly excited.

Soon they all came. There were some horses, all very tall, and some little ponies. Two riders were wearing red coats, just as Silver Queen and Perriwinkle had said they did, and one of them was Ken. With them were lots of hounds—more than he had ever dreamed of. They went in front of Ken's horse. Ken stopped by the gate at the corner of the wood and said something to the hounds, and they all went into the wood. Some riders disappeared along the top edge of the wood behind the trees. One came on through the field towards the gate, which the girl held open for him. As he went through he said:

'Good morning, Jane,'

And the girl replied:

'Good morning, Master.'

Then the man went along the road the way Podge and Jane had come, and waited at the other end of the wood. Podge guessed that this might be the owner of the Great House—his Master in fact, though he had never seen him before. He looked kind, even though he was so important and grand on his big horse.

He could hear the hounds crashing through the undergrowth at the top of the wood, just as Dorothy and Doctor had so often done at home in the Big Wood. He wondered if either of them was there today. Birds flew up out of the trees in alarm as they gradually came down towards the lane. Podge and Jane waited.

Then, without making a sound, a foxcub suddenly emerged from the edge of the wood quite close to them, looked hard at Podge, and hurried across the road and through the hedge on the other side. Neither Jane nor the Master had seen it. Podge gave a sharp bark and tugged at his lead, trying to make Jane realize what had happened.

78

She only patted him and looked along the road; but of course there was nothing there. But the Master caught sight of the cub as it ran off across the field beyond the hedge, and called to her:

'One over there, look. I expect that's why the dog barked.'

The hounds were coming closer all the time: one of them suddenly gave a deep cry, and soon the others had taken it up. They had found the scent of the fox. They made a wonderful noise as they came hurrying through the wood, and Podge wanted to go with them and chase on after the fox as he had once chased scents with his friends Dorothy and Doctor. He rushed forward, but was brought up with a jerk by his collar. He twisted and turned and pulled, but it still held him back. By now the hounds were close and he was mad with excitement. He pulled forward, and it held; sideways, and it held; and backwards, and it shifted, because it was a little loose, moving up to just behind his ears. One final tug backwards and the collar was off over his head, just as the first of the hounds scrambled over the ditch at the edge of the wood and rushed across the lane.

Before Jane could stop him Podge had run across too, squeezed through the hedge and was running among the hounds across the field. It felt marvellous. None of them said anything to him: they were much too intent on their work, and galloping along after the scent. Podge didn't care: he was so pleased to be free and running with them.

In the corner of the field they checked, and he bumped up against Dorothy. She only gave him a quick glance— her nose was to the ground—but she waved her stern:

'Nice to see you,' she said breathlessly. 'Good chap!

Glad you made it. Of course you shouldn't really be with us, so you'd better make the most of it! Come on!'

Podge never forgot the thrill of the run that followed, though at the time everything went so fast that it was all hazy and jumbled. He remembered the speed of the hounds, and how he had galloped and panted and strained every muscle to keep up with them; he remembered the rushing grass, the hedges they had scrambled through,

the ditches they had waded through; he remembered the prickles, the burrs in his coat, the feel of the wet grass under his paws, the air rushing past him, the strong smell of the fox; he remembered the sounds of rustling and cracking and splashing and horses' hooves pounding behind them, and the wonderful sound of the hounds in full cry. And he also remembered how he gradually became more and more tired, and how the hounds gained on him and got farther ahead, and how he struggled to keep up with them but couldn't.

At last he simply had to stop. He was panting furiously and he felt as though he couldn't run another step. He was bitterly disappointed. He lay down in the middle of a field and chewed grass, gratefully licking up the dew from it. Then he howled. He so wanted to catch up, but he would never be able to. He just wasn't built like a hound.

After a few minutes he realized that he didn't know where he was. He didn't want to go back the way they had come, and he thought that if he followed the scent of the hounds he might perhaps eventually find his friends again. This time he would have to go at his natural speed.

It took him quite a long while. He trotted doggedly on over the fields—and they seemed huge now—pausing where the hounds had paused, going on where they had not hesitated, going over or through or under as and where they had. He had no idea how long it was taking him, though he felt that the sun was getting much hotter, and the dew was almost gone. After a while he lost the scent of the fox, and could smell only hounds. Evidently they had lost it too. He came to a tangle of rough bushes and brambles and a few trees, and had a difficult time trying to find where the hounds had left it, still without the scent of a fox, though he had come upon the scents of two in his search. It seemed that the hounds had not managed to scent them and they had escaped.

Then he followed them to a series of long thick hedgerows where a fox could hide quite easily; and after working his way along them he came out at last through a gateway into a big field, with a small wood on the left. At the far end of the field he saw what he had been looking for.

The riders were in a group, resting on their horses, talking among themselves and to Jane. Podge felt very apologetic—he had completely forgotten her. He hoped no-one would be cross with him for running off and trying to be a hound. The hounds—Dorothy among them —were clustered round Ken, some standing, some sitting, some lying down, some scratching themselves, others rolling in the grass. It seemed that the hunt was over. Podge trotted towards them, very tired but very pleased.

Dorothy saw him first, and came racing across to meet him.

'Good old Podge!' she said. 'You *have* hunted well. Doctor will be so cross he's missed you. He stayed at home today.'

'I really wished I were a hound,' Podge replied. '*And* I wished my legs were longer! You went so *fast*!'

Everyone had seen Dorothy dash away from the pack, and so saw who it was she had gone to meet. Jane gave a delighted cry:

'Oh, Podge, I'm so glad you're not lost.'

'Lost? Him?' said Ken with a chuckle. 'Not likely, Miss. He followed that scent all the way till he found us again. That's a real good little 'un, isn't he, Sir?'

'He's keen all right,' said the Master, sitting at ease on his tall horse. 'Isn't he one of ours? He looks quite a useful terrier.'

Podge adored being the centre of attention, with Jane patting him and saying how clever he had been and with all the hounds taking to him and asking questions and

admiring the way he had managed to keep up with them for so long. He thought that hunting was a very good thing, that hounds were the nicest and best sort of dogs next to terriers, and that Ken and the Master were the sort of masters that dogs should have, even though he liked Jane better. He felt tired but very, very pleased with himself. Altogether it had been a most satisfactory morning.

The Great House

In which there is another parting and Podge makes an important journey

ODGE could hardly wait to get home and tell Minnie and Manager all about his exploits at the hunt. He trotted impatiently beside Jane, tugging on the lead, and when they reached the cottage and her parents had been told all about it he rushed to the farm as soon as he decently could, eager for more praise. As soon as he came into the yard he was greeted by an irate Minnie.

'And where were you this morning?' she scolded. 'Evadin' the work as usual? It won't do, will it now? I mean, you must learn to take some responsibility now you're older, and pull your weight. We've seen too much of this behaviour of yours lately.' And she sniffed angrily. 'It didn't occur to you that Manager and I had to do all the work by ourselves, now, did it?'

Podge was cross, disappointed of the sort of welcome he had expected.

'All right then,' said he. 'I won't tell you about the Hunt, then. I was appreciated there, anyway.' And he stalked off across the yard with injured dignity.

Minnie rushed after him. 'Did you say "Hunt"?' she

asked. 'Where? When? What happened?' Then she saw Manager in the distance. 'Manager, Come here! Magpie's bin out huntin'!'

Podge laughed to himself to see how impressed she was, and proceeded to tell both Minnie and Manager all about it. He exaggerated a little, and he didn't say just how small and young the cub had been. The important thing was that *he had been hunting*, and that both Ken and the Master—*and* the hounds themselves—had said how good he was.

After this Podge lived in a glow for some days, respected as he had never been before by the older dogs, especially by Minnie, who thought very highly of such social achievements (Manager was not impressed by this in the least: what he admired was the way Podge had kept up with the hounds for so long), and who was delighted that Podge had shown himself such a worthy member of the Family. In fact, she began to talk more about the Family, telling stories of her puppyhood at the Great House, repeating what the older dogs had told about their hunting days, and talking with familiarity about the exploits and characters of the various hounds (though she had never actually seen any of them, only heard about them from others!). She also began hinting that after this Podge might expect a distinguished future.

'You have made your mark,' she said, 'Like I always said you would. It will not go unnoticed. Give it a week or two, and something will be done. I always did say that breeding would tell.'

Podge was impatient of such talk—he knew Minnie's superstition and snobbery too well. But, all the same, he felt a sort of suppressed excitement, and without realizing it spent the next week or so waiting for something exciting to happen.

And of course it did. Minnie had been right again. One fine afternoon there was the sound of hoofs clattering up the stony lane, and into the yard rode the Master on his tall horse. He pulled up in the middle of the yard. Manager rushed out, barking, as usual at any strange sound, but stopped abruptly when he saw who it was, and wagged his tail instead. The noise brought out Minnie and Podge, who had been mousing quietly in the barn, and attracted the attention of the farmer, who soon came out from the stable where he had been feeding the calves.

While the Master talked with the farmer the three dogs stood looking at him, admiring him, and comparing with the horses they knew his elegant brown mare with her fineboned legs, her aristocratic face and her long black tail which she flicked gracefully at the occasional fly. She played gently with her bit and shifted her feet impatiently. The Master took no notice, but went on talking to the farmer, sitting relaxed in his saddle, looking as though he grew there. Both men looked frequently at Podge as they talked.

This did not escape Minnie's notice.

'Told you so,' she said triumphantly. 'I said something would happen.'

'You may be right at that,' agreed Manager grudgingly: he always hated to admit that Minnie could be right.

They waited for something to be said which would confirm their suspicions. At last the farmer said:

'Yes, well, in a kind o' way I shall be glad to see him go —he'll be happier with that kind of life, I think, and to tell you the truth, Sir, since the hounds went he's fretted, and he sulks, if you take my meaning—doesn't co-operate. In fact, he can be a downright nuisance at times.'

'I think he could do quite well,' replied the Master. 'He seems quite a bright, keen sort of dog. But as you say, he needs a job to do.'

So he was going to the Great House after all. Soon he would be hunting. Podge could hardly believe that what he had wanted so much should really be going to happen. He felt a sudden wave of sadness at leaving the farm, which was the only home he knew, and at saying goodbye to Minnie and Manager, who had been his teachers, comforters and friends. He would miss them.

The dogs sadly said goodbye, as they had done before not so very long ago when Dorothy and Doctor had left.

'We'll be thinking of you,' said Minnie. 'Mind you visit us now and then, and don't let us down.'

'Best of luck,' said Manager gruffly.

Then the Master gathered his reins together, turned his horse, said goodbye to the farmer:

'We'll hope he'll follow me,' he said. 'If he won't, I've got a lead; but I rather think he will. Come on, Magpie! Come with me!'

Podge didn't hesitate. At the sound of his proper name, used so rarely at the farm but through Minnie's stories and instruction associated in Podge's mind with the Family, the Great House and the Hunt, he obeyed at once, and followed the Master out of the yard and down the lane, at that moment feeling almost no regret, only a bounding sense of excitement and importance.

He had to trot briskly to keep up with the long strides of the mare. She looked round from time to time to see how he was getting on.

'Not too fast, I hope?' she asked. 'You'll soon get used to it, anyway, out on Exercise.'

'No, it's fine,' answered Podge. 'I'm used to keeping up with Dorothy and Doctor. They're hounds,' he added as an afterthought. 'They were walked here.'

The brown mare listened courteously. 'It's a good life,' she said, 'If you don't mind company, that is. The Club's very comfortable—old-fashioned, if you know what I mean—regular life, decent food, plenty of exercise and so on. Or so I'm told.'

The Club. It did sound grand. Minnie had often described it to him: the rows of kennels, each with its little yard, the main room and the larger yard, the view onto the drive where they could see everyone coming and going. And the terriers, his family, in their hierarchy with his father, Matchbox, at the head, then the various grades of other dogs—brothers and sisters, cousins, uncles, aunts and other relatives—each with his or her clear position in the order of precedence. A fearsome society, tightly knit, conscious of its privileges and its authority. Podge found himself wondering how he would fit in. Would the others accept him as a member of the Club?

The Master looked round at him from time to time and said something encouraging. His face was kind though full of authority, and Podge began to understand a little what the hounds felt about Ken—a mixture of affection and awe.

They crossed the familiar fields and went up the hill to the edge of the wood. There they went through a little narrow hunting gate and up a small track onto the big ride. They turned briefly right along the edge of the wood, not far from where Podge had had that memorable

meeting with Sir Charles, and then picked up another
ride which cut straight up through the wood.

Podge had never been as far into the Big Wood as this:
it was all forbidden territory for the farm dogs. Now he

could follow the brown mare with a lordly air, feeling as
though he owned it all. The ride was wide and grassy,
edged on one side by tall trees—pines and elms and oaks
—and on the other by a plantation of young trees, fenced
in to prevent animals such as rabbits or deer from

damaging them. Bright autumn sunlight shone onto the ride through the trees, dappling it with flecks of shadow. After some distance they came to a grassy place where six rides met, marked in the centre by an old stone column. They crossed over, taking the ride almost opposite, and could see the Great House itself framed between the trees at the end. From now on, Podge thought, this was to be his home.

II

The Club

In which Masters performs the introductions and Podge leads a new life

HILE Podge waited impatiently outside, the Master put his horse in the stable. Then he came out and Podge followed him eagerly round the corner to the Club. It was just as Minnie had described it: a row of comfortable-looking kennels facing the wall of the stable block and the drives, with neat yards enclosed by black railings. It looked welcoming. As they approached, all the dogs rushed out and stood in their yards barking. Podge felt rather taken aback, and somewhat apprehensive. Perhaps it was going to be more difficult than he had expected. There were so many of them: black and white, brown and white, long-legged like Manager or short-legged like Minnie. They fell silent as the Master opened the door into the main yard and took Podge in, closing it behind them, and they all looked Podge up and down. No-one said anything. They wagged their tails at the Master, but gave no sign of recognition to Podge. Clearly they were waiting for a lead from Matchbox before they did so.

One kennel was empty. It was the third from the end nearest the drive. Into this the Master put Podge.

'Good luck, Mags,' he said. 'I'll come back later.' Then he closed the door and went away.

Podge looked around him. On one side of him, his left, were two young dogs, almost puppies, like Minnie in size but mainly white. The dog had almost no brown on him, the bitch several brown patches and a brown head. They looked friendly, and their tails just quivered in greeting. In the kennel on the right were two long-legged dogs, brown and white. They were very alike, the bitch smaller than the dog. Podge suddenly realized with delight and relief that he had met the dog before: it was Masters, whom he had rescued from the earth in the Big Wood on that stormy winter night. Thank goodness he at least knew someone.

'Mornin', Magpie,' said Masters. 'Nice to see you here. Hoped you'd come. Glad you made it.' Then he put his head close to the bars and added: 'It'll be a bit sticky at first, but don't worry. That's old Matchbox—*you* know, always a stickler for protocol. But then, he was brought up in the old school, where it came naturally. All the others follow his lead, of course. Stuff and nonsense, I call it; but you'll have to watch your paws for a bit. I'll vouch for you. In fact, I'll introduce you to the old boy now. Don't show you're scared, whatever you do, and do answer up. He can't stand ditherers.'

'Oh, thank you,' said Podge gratefully. He wondered what it was about his father that made him so terrible, and gave him such a reputation. He remembered that even Manager had heard of him.

Masters coughed apologetically. Podge looked past him to the end kennel, the one which had the commanding position nearest the drive. In the yard, standing stiffly by the bars, was Matchbox, an old and very grizzled warrior, with a thick, rough, black and white coat, a black head with a white stripe like Podge's own, and large, glowing, amber eyes. He looked very stern,

and his nose was covered with scars from the numerous battles he had fought. Beside him stood a small, delicate, brown and white bitch with a thick coat and a long tail. She looked encouragingly at Podge.

'Sir,' said Masters. 'Allow me to present Magpie. I think I can vouch that he will be a valuable member of the Club. (Bin walked by Minnie an' Manager—good solid provincial education an' all that.) Met him one night last winter when I was out huntin'—filthy night—got stuck down an earth y' know.' (At this some of the younger dogs sniggered, but Matchbox silenced them with a look.) 'Magpie dug me out. Pretty good show for a puppy, as he was then. Dash bad scent that night—used his brains and fetched some hound friends of his to find where I was. Resourceful, I call it. I wouldn't be here now but for him.'

Matchbox looked Podge carefully up and down for what seemed a very long time. Finally:

'Hm,' he said. 'Harrum . . . Mornin', Magpie. You seem to have done credit to the Family. I think the Club could use a member like you.' He paused, then added with a slight air of embarrassment: 'Er, glad to see you. Hope you settle down all right.'

'Thank you,' said Podge, 'Thank you, Sir.'

Matchbox inclined his head slightly to indicate that the interview was over, and returned stiffly and with great dignity into his kennel.

Everyone was relieved. 'That went off well,' said Masters. 'Better than I expected, in fact. The old man seemed quite pleased. Now let me introduce you to the others. First, meet Amber.'

Amber was the shaggy brown and white bitch who shared Matchbox's kennel. Unlike the other terriers, she had a long tail. Podge later learnt that she had been very ill as a puppy and so it had not been docked as is usual with terriers. She was much more friendly now that Matchbox had gone. 'You did very well, my boy,' she said.

Sharing Masters' own kennel was Marigold, his sister. On the other side of Podge were Sting and Sprite. They were about Podge's own age and very envious of all his experience. Beyond them again was a plain and solid-looking cousin called Sponger, who shared a kennel with Starlight, Podge's mother. She was very like Podge, but her markings were brown whereas Podge's were black. She was very pleased to see him after so long, and proud of the way he had 'turned out' as she put it. 'I'm glad you've come back,' she said. Podge decided that he liked her very much, although of course she seemed less like a mother to him than Minnie, whom he had known from a puppy and who had brought him up.

Then there were the others: Shifty and Shady, Spinner and Splash, Truant and Trouncer. They had kennels down the other end of the block. They were all relations of one kind or another, and they all regarded Podge appraisingly to make sure that Matchbox had been right in passing him for membership of the Club. Podge was very conscious of the honour that had been conferred on him, and of the professional standards that he would have to live up to.

In the days and weeks that followed Podge settled into the Club routine, though he found it at times a little irksome. First thing in the morning they were taken for a brisk run in the Big Wood by some member of the Great House family while their kennels were swept and fresh straw put down. Then they went back again, perhaps only for a short while if the Master was going out that morning, or perhaps for longer if their Exercise was to be in the afternoon. Exercise sometimes meant following the Master or one of his family on foot; but more often it meant following his horse as he rode round the countryside visiting various parts of his estate or calling on friends. At no time did Exercise mean dawdling and leisurely exploration such as Podge had been used to at the farm: the dogs were expected to keep together and to follow the horse closely without having to be called all the time. If a dog got left behind or stayed investigating something without instructions to do so he or she had to make his own way back home, and both the Master and Matchbox could be guaranteed to tell him off when he returned.

After Exercise the dogs would go back in their kennels. In the evening they were fed—good, nourishing, old-fashioned food as the brown mare had said. Then they were taken for another brisk run in the Wood and then shut up for the night.

It was after dark that the Club came into its own. Though the dogs had separate kennels for sleeping in, there was behind them a single larger room where they could go if they wished. In this lounge there were benches upon which they sat in the long winter evenings after the day's work was done, and here they would chat, recounting incidents of the day's exercise, gossip they had gathered from outside friends or acquaintances or had

overheard from the Great House people or the hunt staff, adventures of the day's hunting if they had been, or reminiscences about the past. Matchbox always sat on his accustomed bench, and it was one of the rules that whenever he talked all other conversation should stop. Amber sat beside him, asleep most of the time, for she was getting old, and unlike all the others she was privileged to sleep even while Matchbox talked. Every so often she would wake up and say, 'Yes, certainly,' or 'Of course, dear,'—usually in the appropriate places—before falling asleep again almost immediately.

The puppies simply listened to whatever anyone else said, taking in even the tallest stories as fact. Some of the

8   AP

older dogs sat talking lazily among themselves, dozing perhaps from time to time or cleaning their coats in a desultory fashion. Among the younger dogs who were struggling to establish themselves and seeking to better themselves in the hierarchy—dogs like Trouncer, Spinner and Sponger—there was much cross-talk and telling of tall stories, each trying to go one better than the others. They would begin talking in undertones as soon as Matchbox began to doze, and soon the talking would get louder and louder, sometimes finishing up as a quarrel. When it began to get noisy one of the older dogs would intervene: first Masters, who was second in command, and effective Master of Ceremonies during the evening: then, if he failed, either Amber by her age and gentle authority or Matchbox by his gruff command would put a stop to it, and the offending dogs would be sent to their kennels.

In their corners, the bitches talked quietly and peaceably. They rarely disagreed among themselves; and none of the dogs would ever presume to quarrel with a lady. Such failures in Club manners were severely dealt with and regarded with extreme contempt.

Last thing at night the Master would come to let them out for their run, and then to shut them up. They would gather in the main yard after their run, waiting for the evening ritual of Locking the Gates. It was a ceremony which never varied. First went the puppies, Shifty and Shady and Sting and Sprite; then the pairs of older dogs, Truant and Trouncer, Spinner and Splash, Sponger and Starlight; then Podge, the odd one out; then Masters and Marigold; and finally, in keeping with their rank, the fearsome Matchbox and the gracious Amber.

Podge found the first few nights rather miserable and restless, being the only one with a whole kennel to himself; but after a while he got used to it as he did to all the rest of the strange new life, and he began to enjoy it immensely. The discipline was far stricter than he had ever known or expected, but somehow it wasn't so bad when everyone was in it together and accepted it as the proper thing. He loved trotting importantly along behind the Master's horses on Exercise, or helping the others investigate an earth. He found his kennel more warm and comfortable than his quarters at the farm, and the food more interesting. He liked the regularity of the life, the order and tidiness after the constantly altering pattern of events at the farm, and he preferred having a definite job in life to do to wandering rather aimlessly and doing nothing in particular. And at first he liked listening to the stories the others told, imagining himself doing similarly brave things, and being able to describe them so nonchalantly afterwards to an admiring audience.

On the other hand, he missed after a bit the freedom to go off hunting when he felt like it; and he missed very much his friends at the cottage. Occasionally when he felt carefree and bold he would fall behind the others and hunt a bit on his own, finishing up with a visit to the cottage and a chat with Minnie and Manager. Sometimes he even brought one of the others with him—usually Marigold, whom he rather liked—or occasionally Masters. Then he really was told off when he returned: it was bad enough him going off on his own, but it was even worse to lead one of the others astray; but usually he reckoned it was worth the Master's disapproval or Matchbox's anger just to be free from time to time.

But he still hadn't been hunting. He had seen others go
—Matchbox and Masters went quite often and came back
with fresh scars and new stories, and sometimes one of
the younger dogs would go with them to work under
their supervision and guidance. But some time went by
and still Podge hadn't been. He was very disappointed:
he had so much looked forward to hunting. At last he
called Masters aside one day when they were out on
Exercise, as they lagged behind the others investigating a
hollow tree, and confessed just how disappointed he was.
Masters listened patiently.

'Yes,' he said eventually. 'I quite see your point, Mags.
I'll have to see what I can do. Mind, I can't guarantee
anything. But I'll sound out the old man when I can get
him in a good mood, and see if he'll let you go instead of
one of us one day. I don't think the Master'll give any
trouble: I know he likes to humour the old man—that's
why I think he's waited so long before takin' you.
Wouldn't do to take a new member at once, y' know.
Precedence an' all that. But I'll have a shot at puttin' it
tactfully and we'll hope Matchbox agrees.'

'You are kind,' Podge replied. 'I do appreciate this, you know.'

'Not a bit, not a bit. Anythin' for a good friend,' answered Masters hastily, 'After all, you saved my life.'

'Please don't mention it,' said Podge, embarrassed. There was a pause, then Masters added:

'Come on, we're gettin' left behind. We'd better hurry or neither of us will be goin'.'

12

Hunting

In which an ambition is achieved

ODGE'S chance came a few days later. In the evening Masters came up to him while they were waiting for the Master to shut them up for the night, and said quietly:

'It'll be all right for tomorrow.'

'Really? You mean I can go hunting at last? Doesn't Matchbox mind? Are you sure?' asked Podge all in one breath.

'No, it's quite all right. Actually I don't think he'd mind a day off—feels his age a bit now and then,' explained Masters. 'And this damp weather lately has given him a touch of his old rheumatism. Always gets it at this time of the year, poor old boy. Anyway, let me explain our plan. Matchbox has said he'll co-operate, so it's just a question of manoeuvrin' the Master.' He explained carefully what Podge was to do the next morning, finishing just as the Master's step was heard outside the door.

'Can't say any more,' he concluded hastily. 'Good night to you. And don't forget.' And he went off to greet the Master at the door as usual.

Podge hardly slept at all that night, he was so excited.

Would they be able to bring off their plan? and what would hunting really be like now that he was a member of the Club and not an outsider any more? He slept fitfully, turning on his straw bed but never really making himself comfortable, hearing through the wall the other dogs breathing peacefully as if it were just an ordinary night and nothing important was going to happen.

All night the wind howled and the trees swayed and were swept helplessly around in its gusts. Podge could hear it quite clearly: it made him more and more excited. In the morning he woke long before the others. He went

out into the yard and looked around. It was cold and there was a thick mist wrapped in frayed layers around the trees in the Big Wood across the other side of the drive. Their trunks disappeared into it, and odd elm branches or tufts of pineneedles emerged farther up in unexpected and irrelevant places. The wind had died down a little. Everything was very quiet at first, and then the back door of the Great House opened and the Master came out, pulling on his coat. He came past the kennels, walking with quick nervous strides and shivering a little in the cold air. He looked hard at Podge as he went by, then disappeared into the stable yard. A minute or two later he drove out in the landrover which he always took hunting.

Then he returned to the kennels and let himself in through the gate into the main yard. He went to Matchbox's yard and called him; but Matchbox didn't come out. Then he opened the door of the inner kennel and called again, and a faint growl was the only reply.

'Drat the dog,' exclaimed the Master. 'I don't believe he wants to come.'

By this time all the other dogs had woken and come out into their yards, where they stood watching. The Master let Masters out, and stood thinking for a moment. Now Podge acted according to the plan, and jumped up against the bars of his yard, making as much noise as he could. As they had expected, this attracted the Master's attention. He gave a short laugh.

'All right,' he said. 'At least someone wants to go! We'll have you instead.' And he opened the door and let Podge out. Then he went back into the house again.

'Splendid, Mags,' said Masters. 'Just what I intended, an' it all worked out accordin' to plan. Just watch me

when we're there and I'll soon teach you the hang of it.'

They waited eagerly at the back door, keeping well away from the peacocks, which were by now awake and stepping with cautious and elegant strides round the yard, waiting impatiently to be fed. Noises came from inside the house, and eventually the door opened again and out came the Master, now completely ready in his black cap and string gloves and carrying his hunting crop with its long thong doubled up in his hand. He also had two collars and chains, and with the other hand he

carried the box of coffee cups and thermos flasks for afterwards.

Masters and Magpie followed him to the landrover and climbed into the space at the back which contained sacks and tools and the spare wheel. On each side of the central well was a raised seat over the wheels, and on these the dogs sat, Masters on the right with his head on the Master's shoulder, and Podge on the other side looking out of the window. They waited a few minutes with the Master looking anxiously at his watch, and then suddenly they saw Jane running up, very out of breath and full of apologies for being late. Podge was thrilled to see her:

it made this already exciting day even better. He copied Masters and rested his head on her shoulder.

Podge had never been in a car before. He found it very exciting, watching the hedges and fields rushing by faster than anything he had ever seen, and he loved the feel of the air blowing in at him through the open window. Every so often he looked round at the others to make sure it was all really happening.

They drove on for some way along narrow twisty lanes. Podge had explored much of this country with Dorothy and Doctor: then his view had been bounded by the hedgerows—filled now with tossing teazles and trailing Old Man's Beard—but from the high vantage-point of the landrover he could now see to the fields beyond and the sweeps of rolling country spreading out into the far distance, where they met the forest that ran along the ridge at the edge of the Vale. Everything was very clean-washed after the wind and the rain, and the mist had almost lifted, leaving only a few patches down by the streams and in the hollows and dips. It was all very familiar, yet today it felt different.

Presently they reached country that was strange, and soon they came into a village. They turned off down a little lane, bumped along round several sharp corners and came at last into a white-washed stable-yard, full of people and horses and dogs. Ken was there, and the big brown lorry. Podge very much wanted to talk to the other dogs, but Masters restrained him. 'We're here on Business!' he admonished severely.

Thumpings and bumpings indicated that the trailer and horses were being fixed and loaded; Ken climbed into the cabin of the brown lorry, with Jack the Whip beside him, and the little procession left the yard on its way to the Meet.

It was a long drive, and despite his excitement Podge felt himself falling asleep. He stared hard at the back of the brown lorry, but gradually it became blurred and faded away. Eventually he woke up to find that they had stopped just outside a village. Around them there were people on horses nervously arranging themselves, clutching bunches of reins and chattering to each other, while their mounts sidestepped and dithered and went backwards into each other with their ears laid crossly flat against their heads and their tails switching. There

was a good deal of noise, what with all this and the scraping and thudding of horses emerging from trailers. Podge and Masters were alone in the landrover.

Through the crowd of riders and people on foot Ken and Jack could be seen by a sign-post on a patch of grass, with all the hounds clustered round them. There were noises from behind as the Master's horse was unloaded and the box unhitched. Eventually he rode past the land-rover and joined Ken and Jack. Podge got more and more excited. Surely something would happen soon. But the chatter went on. People came and went; stray hounds pottered off investigating things and were sternly recalled; the crowd got thicker; the horses got more nervous.

Eventually Ken swung round and rode off along the side-road with the hounds fanning out round his horse's hoofs. Jack and the Master followed, and after them the whole throng of eager horses pushing and barging and tugging at their reins: tall elegant horses and little fat shaggy ponies tossing their heads, all as excited as each other. Behind them went people on foot—children wheeling bicycles, farmers in boots and with sticks, round country women in thick coats and with baskets, tiny children clinging to their hands. Jane came puffing through the crowd and flung herself into the driving seat. Then she started the engine. It had begun.

13

Sir Podge

In which our hero is gloriously distinguished

 HE day did not go quite as Podge had planned. He had imagined himself being called for urgently—Masters would be sent after the fox first, of course, but would have failed to bring it up—he would be sent down, and after a long and bitter struggle he would succeed. Everyone would be very pleased with him; he would go back to the Club covered with scars and tell his story—modestly, of course—to the other dogs; and eventually Matchbox would growl, half-reluctantly: 'My boy, the Club is proud of you. You have brought credit to the Family.' And the farm dogs would get to hear of it, and Minnie would say: 'I told you so.' And Manager, not to be outdone, would imitate the farmer and reply: 'I always did think he'd turn out to be a useful kind of dog— useful, that's what,' just as though it had all been his doing. But it wasn't quite like that: in fact, it wasn't like that at all.

It began rather badly. They stood outside a smallish squarish wood which lay on the slope of a hill with a stream running through a piece of bracken-covered ground along one edge. In the field at the edge of the wood, beyond the bracken, the horses and riders waited. Jane and the dogs stood at the top corner by the bracken. Jack was at the far top corner opposite them, and Ken down at the bottom end in the dip by the railway line. In the wood the hounds searched, barging through the thick undergrowth, speaking from time to time in short

bursts. They were working down towards the bracken side, and Ken was coming up along the edge of the wood, keeping as close to them as he could.

Then Podge saw it: a rusty brown shape that loped casually out of the wood and away through the bracken to their right. He barked sharply, tugging at the chain. Jane saw the movement where the bracken fronds were stirred, and pointed. A rider behind them cantered away up the slope to cut the animal off and stop it escaping.

Ken leant forward and came racing up the hill, urgently calling his hounds:

'Here, tally ho! Here, tally ho! Here, tally ho!' Only Podge had actually seen the creature.

And then, frightened by the horseman who had successfully turned it, it broke cover, rushing out from the bracken and dodging within a few feet of Ken before escaping across the field. It was a hare.

'Podge!' said Jane severely. 'How could you?' And Masters growled disapprovingly.

'You'd best buy that dog of yours some glasses, Miss,' said Ken as he passed. 'Jugged hare may do for your supper but it won't earn me my wages!'

Podge kept very quiet for a long while after this. He was very ashamed, but at the same time a bit defiant. It was all very well for Masters to say that he should have known from the way the animal moved whether it was a fox or a hare, but it had all happened so quickly—and why hadn't *he* been watching? And why had everyone acted so quickly after his bark? If they'd waited they would have seen it break cover and then they could have judged for themselves. He'd only barked to call attention to it. It wasn't fair to blame him for misleading them.

After this things went better for a while. The hounds were sent back into the wood and soon found the scent of the real fox, which had crossed the railway and had set off across the fields for West Wood, which sprawled across the slope about half a mile off on the other side of the valley. Everyone went in pursuit, and the dogs scrambled back into the landrover so that Jane could try to catch up on the nearest road. It was rather fun. From time to time they could see people hurrying along, jumping fences and galloping after the hounds. Then the road would twist and they would lose them for a while, or they would have to stop, open the windows and listen for the cry of the hounds or the sound of the horn, before setting off again in the direction the sound came from.

Sometimes they got out and stood by woods while the hounds drew them, or waited to shut gates, or to put up rails after people had jumped the low ones. In the middle of the day they ate Jane's sandwiches in hasty mouthfuls as they drove along.

The afternoon found them watching at one end of a long large wood, all by themselves in an empty field. The other cars which had been following had disappeared; most of the riders had gone home. It was beginning to get a bit darker and very much colder as it drew near the end of the day. They waited a long time. It was a long while since any sound had come from the wood. Podge began to get bored. Jane was obviously a bit worried. She walked up and down the field, listening. At last she said to herself:

'They must have gone. We must have missed them. Drat!' And she tugged the dogs after her towards the landrover, which she had left in the gateway.

They scrambled in and she backed it round to face the road. It was all very quiet. They listened again. Suddenly Podge heard Ken's horn, very faintly in the distance. Jane didn't seem to have heard it. He barked to draw her attention, and stuck his head out of the window to listen again. Again the horn sounded and again he barked.

'You'd better not be wrong again, Mags!' Jane said, starting the engine. She swung the landrover out onto the road and drove off, glancing quickly across the fields from time to time, looking for Ken. After a few hundred yards they came to a little cart-track on their left, which ran along between the fields. She turned into it and they bumped along at an alarming speed, crashing into the ruts and puddles and sending spray up from under their wheels. The dogs bounced on their seats as the landrover jolted along. Podge felt excited. He hoped that something was going to happen at last.

At last they could see them. Over a hedge to their right. in the middle of a field, were the Master, Ken and Jack and the hounds. They were by themselves. Jack was holding the horses and the Master was keeping back the hounds while Ken investigated something in a bank at the far edge of the field. Jane drove through the gateway and across the field towards them. She stopped the land-rover and got out.

Then it all started to happen. She took hold of the horses, Jack went over to Ken and then came running to the landrover. He took Masters out and left Podge behind. Podge could see Masters being sent down the earth Ken had been investigating, and he became very cross indeed. He wanted to go and join in. As the minutes passed he got crosser still. Obviously Masters was making a mess of it. Any respectable dog would have done something by now. *He* would have done something by now if they'd had the sense to take him instead. They wouldn't give him a chance to prove that he could be useful ('useful, that's what!'). They were judging his ability by the silly mistake he had made earlier. He would show them.

How could he get out? He had seen the Master and Jane opening the windows before—they slid aside if you pushed them. Standing on the front seat he could just reach the window with his nose. He tried and tried, but failed. It was the window which was frustrating him. How he hated it.

Podge lost his temper. He opened his mouth and bit the window. He bit it very hard. There was a satisfying cracking sound, and the thick perspex split. Another ferocious bite and a piece of the window had fallen out.

He jumped up and wriggled through the hole. He was free.

He raced across the field towards the bank, barking, and ignoring Jack's exclamation at the damage. Ken, busy at the earth, saw him, didn't stop to ask how he had got there but called Masters out impatiently and put Podge in the entrance instead.

'You have a go, then, my lad,' he said. 'Only don't go and find us another hare, mind.'

The earth was very dark and damp, and smelt strongly. Podge nosed his way down it, his eyes gradually getting used to the dark. Angry noises were coming from farther down—very angry noises, and ferocious spitting. Then this was what foxes were like when cornered. His chance had come at last.

He crawled purposefully along, his claws dislodging pebbles and earth which fell on the creature below and only increased its fury. The spitting and snarling grew louder, and a pair of immense green slit eyes glared up out of the blackness. Podge remembered the night he had met Sir Charles, and the unwinking green eyes that had watched him in the dark wood. He shivered. Hardly the moment to remember that, he thought rgimly. He went closer, recalling Minnie's words: 'You must not let go.' All right, he wouldn't. He attacked.

His jaws closed on a mouthful of fur. Powerful claws swiped at him. He backed away, coughing and trying to spit the fur out. He had been deceived, deluded, made fun of. It was a *cat*. All right, they'd asked for it!

The sounds of battle came up the earth to the watchers above. They listened admiringly—just as Podge had hoped they would.

'Brave little beggar,' said Ken. 'Masters wouldn't face him.'

'Yes,' replied the Master. 'He's a plucky little devil.'

The noises increased. There was an outraged yelp, a scratching and scrabbling, and from the hole at great speed emerged a draggled, tatttered, battered ginger cat. Somehow it had managed to squeeze past Podge, much to his annoyance. It spat at them and fled.

14

Magpie, Alias Podge

In which there is, after all, a happy ending

SHAMEFACEDLY Podge backed up the earth, his stumpy tail flattened, feeling utterly ridiculous and expecting a stern reception. Everyone was weak with laughter. Ken was spluttering and had to be banged on the back—he had had the biggest shock, being closest to the earth. Masters wagged his tail madly.

'Oh my collar and studs!' he said. 'What an achievement! Think what a story this'll make—go down in Club history—cut the others out completely—Family will love it.'

Podge looked sharply at him as they clambered into the landrover and started to make their way back to the Meet. Was he making fun of him? But Masters, though amused, was admiring, and Podge realized that he had meant it quite seriously. Though a conventional dog, he was the first to appreciate anything or anyone less stuffy than the Club. He had always enjoyed 'slumming' as the others had called their stolen visits to the farm and the cottage, and when accused of keeping low company had said simply 'They're my friends'. That was what counted.

Podge suddenly realized what fun it would be telling this story to the Club. It wasn't what they'd been expecting—it wasn't the sort of glory he'd imagined and hoped for—but it was glory of a sort. After all, any of the others—Spinner or Sponger or Trouncer—could have *caught* a fox . . . They'd all be furious that he had the best hunting story of all. On the whole he felt better. Except . . .

They followed the horses, which were tired now and rather slow, back along the rutted lane and then the main road to the place of the Meet. The hounds trotted solemnly, looking wet and bedraggled, their sterns drooping a little. Jane concentrated on keeping just the right distance behind the horses, not dropping too far behind but not getting within kicking-range, and didn't say anything. Masters went to sleep curled up on a sack by the tools. Podge sat bolt upright on the seat over the wheel behind Jane, staring fixedly over her shoulder at the swaying elegant tails of the horses and the tired jogging backs of their riders as they sat loosely in their saddles. He had plenty of time to wonder what they all thought of him.

When they reached the place of the Meet again there was all the tidying-up and putting-away to be done. The hounds were called into the brown lorry and shut safely away. The horses were rugged up and put in their boxes. Hats were taken off and put away and overcoats put on over the beautiful red coats. Then at last it was time for coffee. The three men stood leaning on the landrover while Jane got out the coffee-box. She arranged everything on the bonnet and poured out while Jack handed round the biscuit-tin. They warmed their hands on the cups and started to relax. The two dogs were let out for a run and came cadging biscuits. Ken gave one to Podge and chuckled:

'We'll make him a medal,' he said. 'There isn't another dog like him.'

'Too right,' said Jack. ''E's a beagle, a—a burglar an' a cat-catcher all in one,' he added, with an unusual stretch of imagination.

They laughed.

'But what about you?' asked Jane, looking at the Master, who had been silent and rather abstracted. 'I mean—well—do you mind? Will you let him hunt again—he does love it so. And he does try,' she added loyally.

The Master didn't answer at first. Instead he poked round in the front of the landrover, and after a search

emerged with an old envelope and a rather chewed stub of pencil.

'Well,' he said, resting the envelope on the bonnet and scribbling something. 'I think that rather depends on you —what rhymes with "bark" someone?'

'Mark, shark, hark, spark,' said Jane. 'What do you mean?'

'Lark,' added Ken looking over the Master's shoulder and chuckling.

Jack joined them and grinned. Jane felt rather left out.

'What *are* you doing?'

'You'll know soon enough,' said Ken. 'Take those two for a walk for a bit, will you—then we'll be done all the quicker.'

Jane and the dogs pottered off, somewhat puzzled. There wasn't much to do or see, only three roads meeting, scuff marks and earth from the horses' hoofs all over the road, and hoof-prints on the grass verges. It was nearly dark. Podge and Masters made a half-hearted attempt to put up some birds in the hedge, but they only jabbered at them and rustled onto branches out of reach. Odd snatches of conversation came from the earnest group by the landrover:

'Haven't tried my hand at this since I left school.'

'You can't put all that in one line.'

'Well, you try it, then.'

'Way over the dog's head, of course! Pity, really!'

Eventually: 'I think that will have to do,' said the Master. 'You can come now.'

The dogs tugged Jane back at a run, extremely curious and rather amused at the odd way people behaved.

'I'm afraid this'll have to do instead of a medal,' said Ken, handing Jane a bright round object. 'But it'll be easier to put on his collar.' It was one of the Hunt buttons, which he had just cut off his red coat. It was shiny and gold and had the Hunt's initials embossed on it.

'They can stand for "Matchless and Valiant",' said the Master, inspired.

Jack produced a piece of fine wire and fixed the button onto the ring of Podge's collar.

'My dear chap, what an honour,' said Masters, watching closely. 'That is a Hunt Button—for distinguished service, naturally.'

Podge was beginning to enjoy all this attention. He shook himself and heard the button jingle against the studs on the collar. Obviously they didn't mind what had happened at all—they even seemed pleased. How odd people were. Not like dogs at all.

There was something else. The Master handed the old envelope to Jane with an air of great ceremony. She had to hold it up against the headlight to read it.

'Read it aloud,' suggested Ken. 'Then they can hear it.'

It said: Presented to Jane as an effective Deed of Gift assigning to her from henceforth complete ownership of the dog Magpie, alias Podge, and commemorating the glorious day upon which the said Podge was in succession beagle, burglar and cat-catcher. From his sincere and admiring Friend, Well-Wisher, and former Master.'

'Really, truly?' asked Jane, unbelieving.

'Really, truly,' said the Master. 'He's wanted this all along—to belong to someone properly—and just like a terrier he's got his own way in the end! But read the rest —we had enough trouble composing it! That's with love from all of us.'

So Jane read it.

The Ballad of Podge

This ballad tells the story
  Of the day Podge made his
                          [mark.
He made us think a hare a fox
  With one misleading bark.

He fancied he could do as well
  As his friend Masters. But
When Masters was put down the
                          [earth
  Podge in the van was shut.

He fumed and raged, then with his teeth
  The window did attack.
One bite—another—and it split
  With an almighty crack!

He scrambled out, and speedily
  Went racing to Ken's side.
Masters came up, and Podge went down
  The dark earth gaping wide.

Within the cavern's murky depths
   The fiendish creature lay.
It spat and snarled and hissed and scratched:
   An animal at bay.

Sir Podge he bared his gleaming teeth
   And for the fox he sprang.
But he only bit a cat's soft fur
   While it mauled him with its fang.

O listen ye who do desire
   That all may know your worth:
It's wise to act more modestly
   When going down an earth

Or you may find as our Podge did
   By sad experience, that
One cannot look so dignified
   When worsted by a cat.

His virtues no-one will deny—
   Not swift indeed but stodge.
It's no use being called Magpie
   But wanting to be Podge.

We think he wasn't happy when
   He lived rough on the farm;
Nor was the Club his sort of home,
   Where every bitch is 'Ma'am'.

He wanted to be free to come
　And go, or chase a rabbit;
To have a basket by the fire
　And ordered daily habit.

And so today has been the means
　Of making it quite plain,
That whether
　walking riding hunting stalking
　ratting eating sleeping catting
　(or anything else for that matter)
He'd rather be with Jane.

The dogs listened attentively.

'A worthy ballad,' said Masters after a moment's consideration. 'Doggerel, of course; but adequate of its kind—especially considerin' how quickly they knocked it up.'

Podge wasn't paying attention. He hadn't quite followed it all—some of the words were difficult, but then he hadn't had a sophisticated education like Masters. Anyway, all that really mattered to him was what had come first—he belonged to Jane. Funnily enough, it *was* just what he'd really wanted without knowing it. (How had the Master known?) He would be able to do all the things he liked doing best and be with the friends he was most fond of. He could visit the farm and the Club whenever he wanted and be welcome; he could hunt seriously—or not; he'd have a basket by the fire—and lots of food—and a Family all to himself.

He shook his head to make the button jingle, and squinted down at it, all shiny and gold.

' "Matchless and Valiant",' he thought. 'Or "Misbehaved Varmint",' he added more humbly. 'Makes no odds, as Minnie would say. I've been called both in my time.'

He turned to Masters.

'Three guesses what Minnie will say.'

' "Well, it doesn't surprise me—not at all it doesn't. I always said that puppy had a future." ' Masters replied immediately in a rather squeaky parody of Minnie's accent; and he shook imaginary long fur into place in a conclusive sort of way.

Podge assumed Manager's bored expression and scratched pointedly at a flea.

' "I always did think he'd turn out to be a useful sort of puppy—*useful*, that's what",' he grunted.

'Just look at those dogs,' said the Master, stamping his feet in the cold. 'Anyone would think they were laughing.'

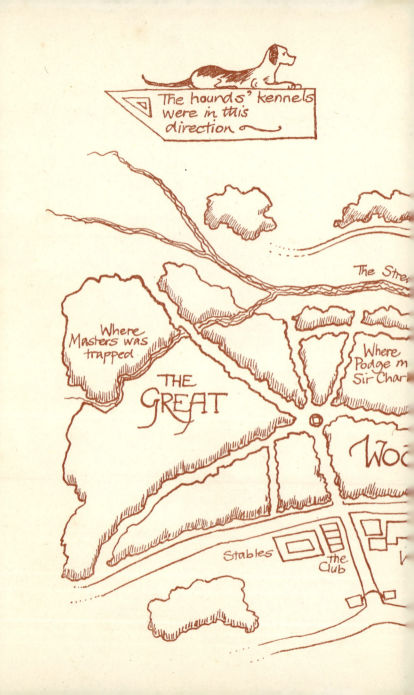

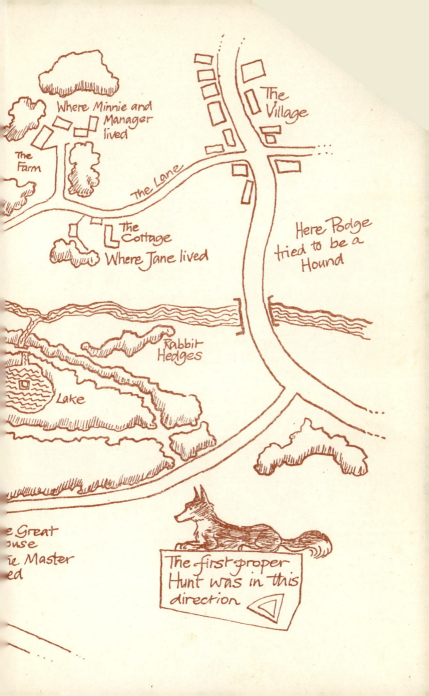

Where Minnie and Manager lived

The Farm

The Lane

The Village

Here Podge tried to be a Hound

The Cottage
Where Jane lived

Rabbit Hedges

Lake

e Great
use
ie Master
ed

The first proper Hunt was in this direction

To: Clare
With love on your 8th Birthday
Aunty Joanne, Uncle Derek &
Richard

Alias Podge